The Year of BIG DREAMS

Karen McCombie

SCHOLASTIC

First published in 2013 by Scholastic Children's Books
An imprint of Scholastic Ltd
Euston House, 24 Eversholt Street, London, NW1 1DB, UK
Registered office: Westfield Road, Southam, Warwickshire, CV47 0RA
SCHOLASTIC and associated logos are trademarks and/or registered
trademarks of Scholastic Inc.

Text copyright © Karen McCombie, 2013

ISBN 978 1 4071 3173 3

A CIP catalogue record for this book is available
from the British Library.

Printed by CPI Group (UK) Ltd, Croydon, CR0 4YY
Papers used by Scholastic Children's Books are made
from wood grown in sustainable forests.

1 3 5 7 9 10 8 6 4 2

This is a work of fiction. Names, characters, places,
incidents and dialogues are products of the author's imagination
or are use fictitiously. Any resemblance to actual people, living
or dead, events or locales is entirely coincidental.

www.scholastic.co.uk/zone

For little F. B., whose name I've borrowed,
since it fitted so perfectly. . .

JANUARY (THIS YEAR)

How it all ended and how it all began. . .

I'm freaked out.

How come?

Maybe it's the fact that the woman opposite us looks like a human lollipop, all skinny body and big face.

Maybe it's because the lollipop lady's face has more make-up on it than all the girls on the make-up counters in Debenhams put together.

Maybe it's because I'm sitting on the uncomfiest "comfy" sofa ever.

Maybe it's because I'm so nervous I could barf.

Maybe it's because I'm about to be stared at by several million people.

Yep, *that's* why I'm freaked out.

(Mum seems to know and squeezes my hand.)

"In. . . Five! Four! Three! Two! *One!*" says a young guy in front of us, large headset covering his ears, hugging his clipboard to his chest.

A switch flicks somewhere inside the lollipop lady and she casts aside her notes and blank expression and positively beams at the camera.

"Welcome back to *Rise & Shine* – the programme that'll brighten up your wintry morning!" she twinkles. "And now we have an update on a story which *gripped* the nation last year. And to tell us all about it is the one and only Queenie Rae Brown, who is here today – along with her adorable daughter Florence!"

Small problem with that intro, Mrs Lollipop. "Adorable" makes me sound like I'm a puppy and my name is *not* Florence.

I sneak a quick sideways peek at Mum, but I think she's secretly freaked out too. Otherwise she'd've jumped right in and let the lollipop lady – and the several million viewers – know that I'm just plain Flo.

Still, this is the first time she's been on telly since . . . well, *everything*, so she's allowed to be nervous, I guess.

"Thanks for coming in to talk to us, Queenie! Especially on today of all days – when *this* year's *Big Dreams* competition launches! How does that make you feel, after what happened to *you*?"

Ouch.

The lollipop lady may have an iridescent coral-pink smile stuck on her face, but it's like she's slapped Mum with her words. Nice start. *Not. . .*

I glance at Mum and silently *will* her to come back all cool and collected.

As if I needed to worry.

She looks . . . *magnificent.*

Her trademark dark beehive is piled high, with a red flower pinned into it. She's wearing a tight, short-sleeved red-and-white gingham shirt, which shows off the trailing roses tattoo on her left arm perfectly. She's swapped her usual jeans-with-turn-ups for cropped black trousers. And her red suede wedges with the ankle straps – they're my favourites.

"It's certainly been a crazy year in lots of ways, Sasha," Mum answers confidently, with a wide, scarlet-lipped smile. "But, yes, *Big Dreams* has certainly had an amazing impact on my life. Well, *all* our lives, eh, Flo?"

Mum looks at me with her beautiful browny-green eyes, perfect swoops of black eyeliner framing them. Those eyes, the dimples when she smiles or laughs, the tattoos, her whole vintage fifties style, the *voice* . . . no wonder everyone – and

I mean EVERYONE – thought she was going to be a worldwide, million-selling megastar.

"Mmm," I squeak and nod.

"*Really?*" says the lollipop lady, whose actual name I'd forgotten in my panic, till Mum said it just now. "But Queenie, yours was hardly a fairy tale with a happy ending, was it?!"

Sasha's attempts at funny banter sound a bit cutting to me. I give Mum's hand a tiny squeeze, one that I hope the camera can't pick up. Though I don't care what any of the millions of viewers think, really. Except, of course, a few viewers in particular, like Freddie and Zee and everyone in Marigold Parade. I know they'll be watching and sending good vibes.

Mum gives my hand an imperceptible squeeze back, with an added tickle of her little finger in my palm, secret code style.

Instantly, I know what she's trying to tell me. Oh yes, Sasha the lollipop lady might think she's been oh so witty there, but me and Mum know the truth. We both know that our year of *Big Dreams* was wonderful and weird, exciting and lonely, amazing and awful, all at once.

And actually there were times when it was a *lot* like a fairy story. That's it; if Sasha asks me how

I felt about the last year, I'd say it was like the tale of Cinderella for sure, only slightly mixed up and mashed up and *kind* of in reverse.

"The thing is, Sasha," I hear Mum say, "I'm a big believer in happy endings coming in all shapes and sizes, and I think I have one now. Even if it's not the one I expected!"

Yes! I think proudly, lost in admiration for my gorgeous mother. There were times in the last twelve months when I was really angry with her and even wildly *worried* about her, but here she is . . . more together than she's ever been.

"Yes, well, that's *one* way of looking at it!" laughs the lollipop lady, pretending to be warm and friendly, but pretty much mocking Mum at the same time.

I'm quietly fuming – and suddenly certain that my fearsome gran Olive will be watching and growling right now – when I realize that Sasha the Sarcastic has turned her attention to *me*.

"So over to you, Florence," she smarms. "I'm guessing you're a typical teenager, right?"

I want to come back at her with some assured, snippy remark like "What exactly is *that* supposed to mean?" But with the spotlight fixed on me, whatever sliver of confidence I have oozes away like melted caramel.

After all, it's not just the millions of strangers and the lovely residents of Marigold Parade who'll be watching, I suddenly, heart-stoppingly, realize. It could be Polly and Heidi and the others too. And yeah, by "others", I'm sort of thinking about Marley. . .

"Uh-huh," I hear myself mumbling to Sasha and her mask of make-up.

"It's just that I'm imagining you and your friends doing typical teen things, Florence," she continues, "like sitting around a computer together, sniggering over funny clips on YouTube."

I have an instant mental image of me and Freddie and Zee giggling at dogs nodding along to their owners playing guitar, or babies falling asleep face first in their lunch.

But so what? What's Sneery Sasha getting at?

"Well, I just wanted to ask you, Florence, what did you make of the world watching *that* clip of your mum on YouTube?" says Sasha. "I'm talking, of course, about the video that's had – let's see – eight million, seven hundred and ninety-eight thousand hits at the last count?"

Without waiting for an answer, she swivels her gaze away from me and over to a monitor. Her perfectly manicured hand waves towards it, indicating that me and Mum are meant to look at it too.

My heart lurches as soon as the image pops up of Mum in silhouette, her hand on the microphone, and we hear the roar of the expectant crowd.

Oh, *I* get it.

Sasha wants me to comment on The Moment. The Moment that my already-famous-by-this-time mum became even *more* famous, for all the wrong reasons.

The moment Mum's big dream went pop.

The moment that I realized this talent show had changed all our lives for ever – just not in the way me or Mum ever expected.

"The final of last year's *Big Dreams* contest," I hear Sasha say as the crowd onscreen hushes and the lights rise on Queenie. "When your mum's dreams tragically ended."

Yeah, so some things ended, I fume to myself, my eyes glued to the oh-so-familiar image on the monitor.

But if you really want to know, Sarky Sasha, some things – some absolutely *brilliant* things – also began. . .

JANUARY (*LAST* YEAR)

Saturday 28th January

"Oooooo-OOOOOOOOO-OOOOOO!!"

That's Mum.

Singing along to the radio as usual, effortlessly hitting the high note at the end of the song with a brush held to her mouth, microphone style.

She gives me a wink of one black-winged eye in the mirror as a clatter of applause breaks out in the hairdresser's. All the old ladies coo and smile and clap, thrilled at the free floor show.

Armando claps too, even though he's got a roller in his hand. He loves Mum, and loves her singing. He knows all the old ladies come to his salon just as much for Mum and her voice as their weekly wash 'n' blow dry.

Someone grabs the handle of the broom I'm sweeping up with and I turn to see Maureen, one of the regulars, her white hair dripping wet as she waits for her makeover.

"Oh, Flo, sweetheart, your mother's a *wonder*! She's better than most of the singers on the radio!"

"I know," I say, proud of Mum, even if she's only a hairdresser in an old-fashioned, local salon in the tatty side of town. "Can I get you another cup of tea?"

"Queenie's wasted on us, Flo my love – she should be on the stage, shouldn't she?" says Maureen, ignoring my question and turning to talk to the rest of Mum's appreciative audience, with their bobbing, white-haired heads.

Well, not *everyone's* appreciative, of course.

As I put aside the broom and head for the kitchenette to put the kettle on (the "Ladies" never say no to more tea) I spot Armando's daughter Valerie and his granddaughter Roxanne exchanging snidey glances over the top of their clients' hairsprayed curls.

Watching them – like I do whenever I'm working my Saturday eleven-to-two slot as general tidier and tea-maker – I can see that they're jealous. Jealous that the clients always ask for Queenie and not them. Jealous that she's a better hairstylist than both of them put together (and an awful lot *nicer* than both of them put together). Jealous of the fact that Armando always bobs his own silvery-haired head along when Mum sings (which is always). Jealous 'cause he calls my mum "Your Majesty".

"Princess!" he calls out to me now.

Uh-oh. That's another eye-rolling look between Valerie and Roxanne. You'd think they were sulky schoolgirls the way they act, instead of grown women (Valerie is forty-something and Roxanne had her twenty-first birthday last month).

With their matching long, straightened dark brown hair, trowelled-on eye make-up and pursed, pink-frosted pouts, they look more like sisters than mother and daughter. "Like the *Ugly* Sisters," Freddie said when we passed by them one day, pinch-faced and smoking outside the hairdresser's.

"Can you make a cup of tea for Mrs Jennings while you're there?" Armando smiles warmly at me, the complete opposite of the female members of his family.

"Sure," I answer him, before slipping through the tinkling beaded curtain and into the tiny kitchen.

Armando's great. And I don't say that just because he gave me this Saturday job, or because he rents the flat upstairs to Mum and me, or because he's

Mum's biggest fan. (Well, someone else is too, but that's another story.)

OK, maybe all those reasons *are* why I think Armando's great, but he's also a little bit like a granddad figure in my life, asking how school's going, how my friends Freddie and Zee are if he hasn't seen them kicking around on the street for a bit, always telling me to keep the change when he sends me along to Zee's parents' shop for biscuits for his "Ladies".

Though I'd never say any of that to my gran. Olive would *not* approve. Men are all right in their place, she says sternly, but they are *not* welcome in our family. (That's *another* story.)

"Flo, honey," comes Mum's voice as she parts the trailing curtain to the kitchenette. "Can you do a tea with two sugars for Nora too?"

"Course!" I tell her, tucking a strand of my flyaway hair behind my ear. I could never have a beehive like Mum's, not for all the hairspray in the world. We tried it once, but my hair's so fine and soft that it collapsed like a mudslide down a mountain ten minutes after Mum had sprayed and pinned it rigid.

As I potter around with the teacups, I pick up a copy of the local newspaper that's spread out on the draining board of the sink.

It's opened up at the horoscopes; probably Valerie or Roxanne was reading that earlier and have just left it for someone else, i.e., *me*, to tidy up.

Me in my rags (OK, jeans and T-shirt) running around after the Ugly Sisters, I smile to myself, tucking the *Herald* under one arm, ready to put it back out beside the pile of magazines on the counter.

"Ooh, Queenie! *Queenie!*" I hear a shout from one of the Ladies out in the salon. "Listen to the radio – they're talking about that *Big Dreams* competition on the telly. You should enter – make Marigold Parade famous!"

There's a titter of excited giggles and "Ooh, *yes*"'s.

"Don't know about that, Maureen," Mum turns and answers, with one shoulder still peeking through the beads.

Too right.

Marigold Parade famous?

I don't think so.

Here's why: "Marigold Parade. . ."

That's the way people always say where I live, with the dot-dot-dot after it and a puzzled look on their face.

The trouble is, our tiny street sounds so

pretty, people imagine it must be by the park or somewhere just as flowery and scenic. They don't picture it as the nowhere-ville it really is, just behind the bus station. I mean, yes, they've all driven along Grey Street: the road that's as dull as its name and becomes the dual carriageway that takes you from our town towards the motorway to London. And they all know the useful but un-beautiful Blackwater Retail Park, stuffed with sofa and sports stores.

What they *don't* see is our tiny street, linking the two.

On a map, it looks like a lane, and is so small the printed words are just an eye-strainingly weeny, shortened

M'GLD

PDE

So if anyone happened to accidentally stumble on M'gld Pde, what would they find?

Pavements lined with cherry-blossom trees and hanging baskets of sunshine-coloured flowers? Nope.

On one side, there's a jumble of tiny modern houses, a sort of retirement complex where the Ladies who come regularly to Hair By Armando all live.

On the other side of the road is a row of shops, which are about a hundred years older than the complex they face.

In order, they go like this:

- Hair By Armando (with me and Mum in the flat upstairs).
- The Beanz Café (owned by Freddie's family, who live above).
- Chowdri's Newsagent (owned by Zee's family, ditto).
- The long-empty shop (with its matching empty flat).
- D.B. Gregory Accountants (with ever-changing students living above).
- Marigold Dry-Cleaners (where Olive works, where Olive lives, one flight up).
- The Tattoo Den (owned by Wolfie, who lives ab—

Hold it.

With Wolfie suddenly in my thoughts, I spot something.

Something peeking out from the short sleeve of Mum's fitted shirt. It's a little red dice, with its six-dotted side facing out. As tattoos go, it's small and dainty compared to the trailing roses on her other arm, but it's looming big-time to me right now.

"*Mum*," I bark, clattering the full kettle down on its base and making the water sloosh out. "When *exactly* were you going to tell me about this?"

"Oh, Flo – don't be angry! It's only little," Mum says, looking like a teenager who's been caught out by a disapproving parent.

It's a waste of time talking to her – it's done. But I'm going to go and have a word with someone who should know better.

Barging past Mum, I stomp out into the salon and say, "Armando – we're out of milk. Just going to get some."

"All right, Princess," he says, though I'm sure he can tell by the scowl on my face that I have more on my mind than an empty carton of semi-skimmed.

Ting! the bell on the door chimes sweetly, as I storm out on to the pavement.

"You all right?" says Freddie, coming out of the Beanz Café, about to put out the chalkboard menu for the day.

"Nope," I reply.

Freddie's one of my two best friends, but right

now I'm not in the mood to stop and chit-chat.

"What's up. . . ?" I hear him ask, but I'm too furious to answer another question.

As I stride on, I hear the squeak of Zee's shop door and her always-surprisingly-deep voice asking Freddie, "Is she OK?"

The empty shop window barely shows my reflection zipping by, the glass is so dusty.

Next, I hurry past the accountant's, with its white, vertical blinds.

In the window of Marigold Dry-Cleaners sits Olive, her plum-coloured bob hunched over her sewing machine, doing repairs for Bernard and Philip, who are busy slipping plastic bags over clothes on hangers. Some sixth sense makes Olive glance up as I hurtle past, and over the top of her glasses she gives a puzzled nod in reply to my quick wave.

And now here I am, outside the last shop in the row. An outline of a gawky girl stares back at me in the glass door, shoulders heaving as if she's about to transform into an avenging werewolf or something.

I push on the Tattoo Den door, but – *clunk* – it's locked.

"With client – please press bell for entry", says the sign. It's printed in an old Gothic-style font, to look serious and important. The joke is, it's not telling the whole truth. Yes, Wolfie locks the door when he has a client in, getting some random bit of their skin inked or pierced in the back room.

But he also keeps it locked so no one walks in and discovers him watching his favourite daytime shows when he's got no customers.

I mean, you can hardly expect some freaky alternative girl to trust Wolfie to tattoo barbed wire around her neck if she's caught him watching something as naff as *Cash in the Attic*, can you?

But whatever, I do what the sign tells me.

A lot.

DONNNGGGGGGGG! DONNNGGGGGGGG! DONN-NGGGGGGGGG! . . .

"Has he done it again?" asks Zee, appearing at my side with Freddie in tow. Instead of one there are now *three* gawky figures being reflected back.

"Yes," I growl.

Inside, I see Wolfie come out of the back room and squint hopefully at the door. With the winter sun behind us, he's probably thinking, "Great –

a whole *bunch* of customers."

But then he sees it's only us, three underage neighbourhood kids, so bang goes a morning's potential earnings.

"Hi guys," he calls out cheerfully, and pulls the door open. "What can I do for—"

"Wolfie!" I yelp. "You *promised* me you wouldn't do any more tattoos on my mum."

I have two problems with Mum's tattoos: first, she always gets them done on the spur of the moment, and second, that spur of the moment tends to happen when she's blue.

I mean, why can't she just have a blowout and treat herself to a family-size tub of Ben & Jerry's? It just seems wrong, wrong, *wrong* to go and spontaneously ink something on to your skin for ever, just 'cause you're a bit fed up.

And though Mum *says* she loves all her tattoos, I don't quite believe her. A couple of months ago I caught her looking in the mirror and biting her lip as she studied the ornate number 3 she had done, to represent the unbreakable bond of her, me and Olive. (*Please.*) "Maybe it shouldn't have been so big," she'd said to me. "Or maybe I shouldn't have got it in a Gothic font."

"Or maybe you shouldn't have got it at *all*," I'd suggested.

It was then that I made Mum vow that she wouldn't rush into a tattoo again, in the hope that – with a little bit of thinking time – she'd never have another one *ever*.

And in case I couldn't trust my mum, I'd told Wolfie about her resolution. He's a nice guy, and didn't take offence, especially since I softened him up by saying it wasn't a criticism of his work, which is very artistic, actually (you should see some of the gobsmacking designs on the shop website).

Though a fat lot of good *that* did, obviously.

"Sorry, Flo," says Wolfie, staring at the ground and scuffing the toe of his chunky biker boot on the tiled floor.

He looks like a schoolkid being dragged in front of the head teacher for writing rude words on the wall in the boys' toilet.

Can you believe it? Short, skinny, thirteen-year-old me, making a towering, tattooed, forty-year-old man go all sorry and scared. It would be funny if I weren't so *mad* at him. *And* Mum.

"But you made me a *solemn* promise to talk her out of having any more tattoos," I remind him.

"I know, I know . . . but she came in to see me the other day and seemed kind of down," Wolfie tries to explain. "She said that this tattoo would help her feel more positive or bring her more luck or something, so—"

I don't bother listening to any more excuses.

I love my mum, but sometimes I get tired of having to act like the adult, sensible one when it comes to her (*and* Wolfie). Whatever's got her down – money worries again, probably – she should know by now that a tattoo doesn't help, and she should know how I'm going to feel about her ignoring her promise to me.

Y'know, I'm suddenly tired of everyone and everything in stupid, small-time Marigold Parade today, where the average age would be about seventy if it weren't for me, Freddie, Zee and Zee's baby brother Roo.

The thing is, I'm *young*.

I don't want to be cross with my mum for doing something thoughtless and dumb.

I don't want to end up acting like a teacher and telling off a grown (tattooed) man.

I don't want to go back into Armando's and see Valerie and Roxanne scowling, or listen to Mum singing, or hear old ladies telling me she should be on the telly.

In fact, all I want is to do what most of the other girls at school do on a Saturday: go to the shopping centre with their mates to talk about boys, to try on clothes and drink milkshakes, and spend their allowances on stuff they don't really need from Claire's Accessories.

But it's not going to happen, since my two best friends are like me, and have to work on Saturdays, if Freddie's parents' café or Zee's parents' shop is busy.

And I can't do it because money is always tight with us and I need what I earn on Saturdays for new shoes, not flowery hair clips or beaded anklets that I'll wear once and then get bored of.

"Flo? You OK?" Wolfie shouts after me as I stomp back towards the hairdresser's and my chores, leaving loyal Freddie and Zee behind, probably wondering what's got into me.

"No," I mutter, shivering as a chilly January wind sweeps along Marigold Parade, this shabby, tucked-away little street where I'm trapped, where nothing ever happens. (Unless you count banned tattoos.)

Oh, to have a fairy godmother who could wave a wand and sprinkle just a *tiny* pinch of fairy dust over the grey pavements and matching slate-roof tiles. . .

"Flo?"

It's Olive. I slow down and turn to face her standing in the doorway of the dry-cleaner's.

She fixes me with a knowing look, reaches out for my hand, and holds it in both of hers.

I wonder if she can read my mind, and sense all the blue-ness sloshing about in there.

"Sweetheart," she says, "Bernard forgot to go to the cash and carry, and there's no loo roll in the staff toilet. Grab us some from the Chowdris', would you?"

I stare down at the £2 coin she's put in my palm.

It's shiny, but it's certainly not fairy dust.

With a sigh, I take the money and head to Zee's shop. Oops – I still have the folded-up *Herald* under my arm; but there's a bin outside the Chowdris', so I'll just chuck it in there.

Except. . .

Hold on.

"Seen something interesting? Ad for a car boot sale? Story about the new zebra crossing by the park?" Freddie jokes, catching up with me and faking a yawn over our dull local news.

"It's – it's . . . no," I mumble, folding the paper up tight and clutching it in my hand.

But I *have* just seen something interesting.

Something that's taken me so much by surprise that I don't know whether to laugh or cry, to be thrilled or worried.

"Flo?" says Zee, appearing by my side and narrowing her dark eyes at me.

"It's nothing!" I say about the Something.

I don't feel able to talk to her or Freddie about this, not while my head is whirring, clunking and fizzling with shock.

But trust me, once I figure out what I'm feeling, my best friends will be the first to know. . .

FEBRUARY

Saturday 4th February

A whole week.

A whole week of knowing about the Something.

A whole week of keeping my secret, not sure what to do about it, or how to *feel* about it.

A whole week of acting normal in front of my friends, in front of my family. *Especially* my family. . .

"And what is *this*?" asks Olive, pointing at the new vase in the middle of the Formica table.

"Beautiful," Mum says, with a beaming smile.

Personally I'm not sure it is. I like a lot of the things Mum collects but this particular vase is very angular and unlovely.

"Hmm," growls Olive.

Olive's flat five doors down is identical to ours (i.e., small) but is full of nothing very much. She likes things minimal, with pale walls and just the occasional framed photo to brighten the place up.

There are times when Olive comes into our packed-with-paraphernalia flat and looks like she's got the beginnings of a migraine.

"More stir-fry, Flo?" Mum asks, blanking out Olive's obvious disapproval of her latest junk shop find.

"Yes, please." I smile up at her. She's looking very pretty; I love the mauve flower she has pinned in her hair today. It matches her purple, paisley, tie-at-the-waist shirt really well.

"More?" she offers my gran.

Olive wrinkles her nose. "Bit heavy on the ginger for my taste."

"Oh, well," Mum says brightly, and goes to walk away towards the kitchenette.

"Hold on! I didn't say I wasn't going to have any," Olive calls out, contrary as ever.

Mum turns with a wicked little smile on her face and a quick wink to me before loading Olive's plate up.

I smile back. I act normal. 'Cause that's what you do when you're squirrelling away a secret you don't want to tell.

BUZZZZZZZZ!

"Huh! Who's that at *this* time of night?" my gran says

indignantly at the sound of the intercom in the hall.

That's pretty funny. It's 5.45 p.m., i.e., not exactly bedtime.

"It'll be Armando; he said he'd pop up after he'd done the till. He's going to have a look at that dripping tap in the bathroom."

"Don't know why he's got to do that when people are having their tea. . ." Olive grumbles, while we hear Mum talking into the speaker, telling Armando to come on up.

"Maybe because he's our landlord, and he comes to fix things as soon as we have a problem," I point out to her. "Which is *kind*."

You have to know how to handle Olive; she's like a grumpy old cat who'll only let you stroke her when she's in the mood – otherwise you risk a claws-out swipe.

And as well as being funny about men, she's protective of her Saturday night tea tradition with me and Mum.

So it's on two counts that Armando has made her hissy this evening.

"Ah, what a *treat*," says Armando, slightly breathless after his jog up the stairs. "All three Brown girls together."

Olive gives him a withering look, though it's a phrase she often uses herself.

"The three Brown girls; all we need is each other" is what she'll trot out from time to time, sounding wise and not-to-be-argued-with.

The three Brown girls. . .

Olive Brown.

Queenie Rae Brown.

Flo Brown.

We're an unbreakable team for sure, even if we don't quite match. My gran Olive (who'd give me a don't-you-dare scowl if I ever called her "granny") is small, round, and plain-speaking to the point of rudeness, sometimes. OK, *often*.

Mum: she, of course, is like a rock 'n' roll butterfly, all fifties fashion and bubbling over with smiles and laughs.

Then there's me. So what am *I* like? Well, I didn't inherit my gran's gobbiness (thank goodness) *or* my mum's style and looks (shame). And I definitely didn't inherit Mum's vocal talents (I sound like a tone-deaf seagull when I sing).

So yeah, that's me: a polite, quiet, little brown moth.

"Hope Queenie isn't planning on going out tonight and leaving *him* here!" my gran hisses over her stir-fry, her chin-length plum bob swinging towards me.

"*Olive*." The tone of my voice warns her not to be rude in Armando's hearing.

Mum's going to the movies with Wolfie later. Olive approves of Mum having a dependable friend like him. Wolfie is most definitely exempt from Olive's man-hate list, possibly because he's such a gentle, goofy giant that hating him would be as silly as hating raspberry ripple ice cream. (Which is for pudding, actually.) Armando's a different matter; Olive likes to think she's the only parent that my mum needs and she resents the fact that Mum sometimes relies on Armando for fatherly advice – and plumbing emergencies.

"Well, he'd better not think he's going to share any of our treats, the silly old man," she adds, with a wicked grin and a wink of her own.

And then I remember why I like her all over again. She brings a different selection of sweets round every Saturday night *and* she can be very *cheekily* funny and make me burst out laughing in spite of myself.

Maybe once we're alone tonight, I should talk to *her* about the Something. Maybe Olive, with her sixty-five years of wisdom, can help me make sense of it.

"Flo – your gum is looking a bit red there," she says, staring me straight in the mouth and stopping my laugh dead. "Have you been flossing properly?"

Then again, maybe I won't bother. . .

Thursday 9th February

"What a dork!"

"Moron."

"What's he like?!"

Those are the rumblings of mutters I can hear, buried in the laughter.

"Freddie!" I hiss. "*Quit* it."

When it's just me, Freddie and Zee, I love all the impressions and fooling around that Freddie does. But in public . . . well, I don't like to think people are taking the mickey out of him.

As for Freddie, he either doesn't hear me or doesn't care.

He's standing on a plastic dinner hall chair, holding the sauce bottle like a microphone and blasting out a high-pitched version of "New York State of Mind".

He can do a mean falsetto for a boy. Just like that old band the Bee Gees. Actually, he's singing it even *higher* than that ten-year-old girl Celeste who won last year's final of *Big Dreams*.

"Freddie!" I hiss again, waving at him to come down.

"You've got no chance, Flo. He's loving it!" Zee laughs, waving a chip along in time to Freddie's crooning.

People always get a surprise when they first hear Zee speak. They see this doe-eyed girl who looks as delicate as a deer, then out comes her husky-as-a-soul-singer voice.

Anyway, she's right; he's not about to shut up, not while all around us students are clapping along, hooting encouragement.

Is it just *me* who can hear the babble of niggly, negative comments?

I glance around to see if I can see who's making them, but there are too many faces. What I *do* notice is Polly Clarke's new hairstyle. She's got long hair that somehow always looks like she's *just* had a blow-dry. And now she's got these subtle highlights done, as if her hair's been sun-kissed in the Med. (Fat chance: it's February, and she's been stuck at school, same as the rest of us.)

"Heidi's earrings are nice, aren't they?" Zee whispers beside me, thinking I'm looking at the rainbow glints of the fake diamond studs in Heidi Webber's ears rather than her friend's new hairdo.

But what am I saying? Like Polly, Heidi lives in Forest Park. If you come from Forest Park, it means you have enough money to live in a big house, to get your hair highlighted as if you've been on holiday, to have *real* diamond earrings if you want them.

Not that Polly and Heidi make a big deal out of living in the poshest part of town. They're OK. There's just this big, obvious-but-invisible gulf between them and us. (Especially the us's who live in Marigold Parade.)

Anyway, they're not the ones bad-mouthing Freddie.

They're cheering him on, actually.

"Whoooo!" Polly calls out, as Freddie theatrically hits the last note and takes a bow, his floppy brown hair falling into his eyes.

"See you on the next *Big Dreams*?" says Heidi.

"Of course!" Freddie jokes, straightening up

and shoving his hair off his face. "Today, Harris Academy dinner hall, next stop, the *Big Dreams* auditions . . . and then world domination! Mwah ha ha ha!"

With that he jumps down from the chair and immediately carries on where he left off with his lunch.

"Nutter," Zee says casually, dipping her chip into a blob of tomato sauce.

"I *know* you are, Zeena Chowdri, but what am *I*?" Freddie teases.

"You shouldn't have done that, Freddie," I mutter. "Some people were laughing at you, and I *don't* mean in a good way."

I'm feeling guilty, of course. It was something *I* said that got him up on the chair, hollering out his song.

I'd been moaning about the February half-term holidays next week; moaning about being stuck doing nothing on Marigold Parade, as usual.

"Where would you most want to go if you could, Flo?" Zee had asked.

"Don't know. Don't mind. . . *Anywhere*," I'd replied vaguely, then remembered the old postcard I'd been looking at this morning. The one in my box, under the bed. "New York, maybe?"

That's what had inspired Freddie to put on his impromptu show, naturally. (Well, *naturally* if you're a goofball like Freddie Rossi.)

"Who cares what losers like that think?" he says now, shrugging.

Freddie's pretty fearless. He may be a bit short and scrawny (and shaggy, with that hair of his), but it's as if he's got Small Dog Syndrome. He's basically a runty little Yorkshire terrier who thinks he's a long-legged lurcher.

"Look, Freddie's fine with it," says Zee. "So why are *you* so bothered, Flo?"

Y'know, now I come to think about it I'm not really sure. All I know is that I've been feeling edgy lately. Fretting over stuff that doesn't matter, because – I suppose – I'm secretly fretting about The Something.

"Earth calling Flo!" Freddie says, waving his hand in front of my face.

I suddenly think again about the box of bits under my bed: the old, tatty New York postcard; a grubby guitar pick; a chunky silver ring with a skull's head; a framed photo of a man in a denim jacket with a fat, freaked-looking baby on his knee.

"Flo, if something's up, *spill*," Zee orders sternly, pointing her fork at me.

I look from one to the other – Freddie's light blue eyes, Zee's velvet brown – and know I *have* to tell them. We've known one another too long to have secrets.

Me and Zee, friends since we were two . . . when Mum and I moved in above Armando's, back when Mum was lost and lonely and with her heart shredded in pieces and a small me to look after.

Five years later, me and Zee became three. That's when Freddie's parents bought the café and he bounded into our lives like he was a puppy who thought we had a stick or a ball he could play with.

So yes, I need to show 'n' tell the Something that's had my head in a knot for too long.

I reach into the inside pocket of my school blazer and pull out a folded piece of newspaper.

"I saw this when I was tidying up in Armando's," I say, rustling the well-folded section of newspaper open.

"'*The Patter of Tiny Hooves*'?" Freddie reads out, sounding confused.

"No!" I say. "Not the story about the new

baby donkey at the petting zoo; look at the story *underneath. . ."*

"Oh."

It's all Zee says, but with that simple "oh" I know that she's instantly understood. (Zee never wastes words.)

Freddie's a couple of seconds behind her.

He reads the headline aloud: "'*Rare Show From Superstars. Thanks to the million-pound refurbishment of the Art Deco Astoria Theatre on the high street, music fans have a treat to look forward to this summer. It's just been announced that legendary band Crimson Hill are playing the first show of their latest tour to celebrate the reopening of this iconic building in June.*'"

I let Freddie absorb the information, and then he gazes up at me, his blue eyes boring into me.

"Does Queenie know yet?"

"I don't think so," I answer, shaking my head. Apart from getting her impromptu and strictly forbidden tattoo a couple of weeks ago, Mum seems to be her normal singing, chatting self.

And as usual, I've been the grown-up out of the two of us, thinking how I can protect her from this particularly HUGE nugget of news.

"Flo, you're going to *have* to tell her," says Zee.

"Think how she'll feel!"

"Olive will be on guard in the street, ready to thwack him with a handful of zips if he comes anywhere *near* your mum!" Freddie says, only half joking.

I let my forehead flop down with a *thunk* on to the table, only semi-bothered by the squidge of sauce I've landed in.

Queenie? Olive? Yeah, it's going to be seriously weird for them.

But what about *me*?

How am *I* meant to feel, knowing my long-lost dad is coming to town?

Wednesday 15th February

A tiny pony.
  My name.
  A black lily.
  A shooting star.
  A red rose.
  Another rose.
  Four more roses, some in bud.
  A butterfly.
  An accordion.

A ladybird.

An ace of hearts playing card.

A dragonfly.

A number 3 in that ornate Gothic font.

And now a dainty dice with its "lucky" six dots.

That's a total of seventeen. That's seventeen times she's been feeling blue and rushed into having a tattoo, like they were permanent mood plasters. I've heard the stories of every one of them – not from her but from Olive, with a sigh and a roll of her eyes.

I'm trying not to notice her newest one now, as she picks up the knife and cuts the flapjack. Since my flip-out at her (and Wolfie) I've just never mentioned it. But *there's* the red corner of it, peeking out from under her puff sleeve.

"Half for you, half for me," says Mum.

Anyone watching might think Queenie has a pretty poor grasp of fractions, since she's shoving at least two-thirds of the flapjack towards me on the antique, floral-edged cake plate.

But that's just her joke; the one she's been doing so long, since I was weeny small.

"Thanks, Mum."

I help myself to my "half" and look out of

the window, watching the Wednesday-morning shoppers drift by.

We're not in the Beanz Café, obviously; they don't do anything as posh as Luxury Fruit Flapjack on vintage floral plates (more sausage, egg 'n' beans on chipped ones). And this bustling street isn't Marigold Parade, since Marigold Parade isn't *ever* bustling and it's *never* full of well-dressed women pushing expensive buggies.

Where we are is Pear Tree Avenue, the main street in Forest Park. Me and Mum, we take a trip over here every couple of months, when Mum's saved up enough of her tips from Armando's in the glass "treat" jar on our kitchen window sill. There's a row of shops here that're a *world* away from ours: an Italian deli nestles next to an organic babywear shop; a shiny estate agent's butts up against a French wine "emporium"; a boutique full of silky dresses is the neighbour of the Woodlands Café where we're sitting now. And dotted between flashy units like these are a couple of charity shops that Mum and me *always* scour for bargains.

We've got bags by our feet now, filled with second-hand clothes from high-street and designer stores we could never afford any other way. We don't care if the sizes or the shapes are all wrong; if the material's right, we have it, knowing that Olive can whirl the clothes into whatever we want them to be on her dependable sewing machine.

Today I got a gorgeous, only *slightly* ripped apple-green cardie and a worn-soft pair of denim dungarees made for someone with legs considerably longer than mine. Not that it matters; I'm going to ask Olive to transform them into a mini dungaree dress. It'll look great with leggings and my stripy long-sleeved T-shirt. *And* the fixed-up cardie.

"So, what do you think, then?" asks Mum, holding a man's short-sleeved Hawaiian shirt up against herself.

"I think you could fit at least *two* of you into that," I tell her, though I know it'll look cute once Olive has nipped it in at the waist and Mum has accessorized it with her wide, black-elastic cinch belt.

"The pattern is just beautiful, isn't it?" Mum sighs, gazing at what I think are hibiscus flowers.

I don't agree with her. Not out loud. I mean, they *are* beautiful, but I can just imagine her showing the shirt to Wolfie and asking him to hammer a copy of the hibiscus into her ankle or somewhere.

"Hey, look," I say instead. "A *sign's* going up."

I'm pointing at the stunning white Regency houses across the road, the ones me and Mum imagine living in whenever we come here. A workman is attaching a "For Sale" sign to a house with shutters and star jasmine growing around the front door.

"Ooh," Mum sighs, dropping the shirt down on to the table. "What a pity we blew my tips on clothes, coffee and a flapjack, Flo. We could've put in an offer to buy the place!"

As she sighs and jokes, I reach over and helpfully lift the edge of the shirt sleeve out of her cappuccino. What would she do without me?

"Hey, Flo!" a voice says suddenly. "What are you doing here?"

I turn around and see Polly Clarke coming in through the café door, followed by Heidi Webber and a boy I don't know.

"Just . . . visiting," I say brightly.

Yeah, visiting the Cancer Research shop for bargains.

"Great," says Polly, and smiles, though she can't take her eyes off Mum. Actually, *none* of them can; Heidi and the boy – who's got a guitar slung over his shoulder – are gawping at the fifties throwback who's sitting right next to me. (Guitar boy; his hair is longer and floppier and somehow *posher* than Freddie's. They could have a flop-off.)

"Um, Mum – this is Polly and Heidi from my year," I say, doing the introductions. "Polly, Heidi, this is my mum, Queenie."

I've missed out Polly and/or Heidi's friend; he must go to another school. One of the two private schools out this way, I bet.

"Uh, yeah, I saw you at Parents' Evening once," Polly says to Mum. "I always wanted to tell you that I *seriously* love your style!"

"Thank you, that's very sweet of you to say," Mum smiles, letting loose her dimples and charming everyone within a ten-metre radius.

"Well, better get a table, I guess," Polly says, now edging away. "See you next week when school's back, Flo."

"Yeah, have a good rest-of-the-holidays," I say back, as I kick the tatty Tesco bag stuffed with my second-hand goodies further under the table.

"Do your friends live around here?" Mum asks as Polly, Heidi and the boy with the guitar settle themselves down at a table near the back.

"They're not my friends, and yes, they do," I mutter. Urgh, the telltale £3 sales tag from the cardie is dangling out of the top of the bag, I notice. (Why does a sales tag have to be so *big*?)

I bend over to tuck it back in and hear the embarrassing jangle of my ancient hand-me-down mobile, with its selection of precisely *one* working sound.

"It's Zee," says Mum, before I can straighten up.

Clunk!

I whack my head on the underside of the table in my hurry to grab the phone before Mum can read it.

"Oh – careful, honey!" says Mum, as I wobble upright. "Are you all right? Seeing stars?"

"A little," I wince, wondering why I was so bothered about Polly and Co. seeing my charity buy when they can now see me doing a fantastic job of looking like a total klutz.

"Well, no worries," I hear Mum reassure me, as I try and shake away the black splodges that are spoiling my vision. "Let's have a look; all Zee's saying is, *Have you told your mum yet?. . .*"

NO!

What am I supposed to say to that?

"Ooh, sounds intriguing," Mum laughs, though

now that her face is coming back into sharp focus, I can tell that there's a twitch of anxiety to her red-lipped smile. "So, er, what *haven't* you told me yet, Flo?"

I am a coward, I admit it.

And Zee and Freddie have been telling me that loud and clear for the last week, since I showed them the piece in the local paper. (Thank goodness for a mother who thinks the *Herald* is just full of stories about burst water mains and faulty traffic lights and doesn't bother reading it.)

"I'm trying to find the right time," I've kept assuring my friends. But the right time always seemed to be just around the corner. Even though I've had a ton of perfectly good opportunities – me and Mum sitting at the Formica table in the kitchen; slouched in front of the telly together; or Sunday morning, when we were curled up in her big bed with toast and magazines, giggling over all the celebrities vying for attention – the words somehow got wedged in my mouth.

"I – I – just. . ."

I feel my face flushing a shade of red that must be nearly as bright as Mum's lipstick.

How do I say it, how do I tell her, how do

I cushion the blow that her no-good ex will be back in town in the not-too-distant future?

"Stop faffing and just DO it, Flo!" I can hear Zee's voice nagging me in my head. "She's got to know!"

I take a deep breath . . . then realize my thirty-seven-year-old mother looks very scared of whatever I'm about to tell her.

Help. If I blurt it out and it comes out wrong, it could send her rushing off to Wolfie and pointing to a random un-inked patch of skin.

I know I need to be the grown-up again, but I'm panicking and I realize that I haven't thought it through properly – even though I've had nothing else rattling around in my brain for the last couple of weeks or so.

I know I'm teetering on the verge of bottling out, but I *can't* do it yet.

Anyway, Dad's not going to be here till June; there's plenty of time to let her know.

I'll just have to think of something that sounds believable for now. . .

And suddenly, there it is – my get-out.

It's right behind Mum, Blu-tacked to the wall, amongst the jumble of other posters for art classes and kiddie gym sessions and stuff.

A glossy ad inviting people to enter this year's *Big Dreams* talent show on TV.

"You're *not* going to like it," I suddenly start gabbling.

"Uh-oh," Mum says, pulling a face. "Do I need to sit down? Ah, but I already am. Drat."

I ignore her efforts at being funny and plough on.

"The thing is, I know you're tired of all the Ladies and Armando trying to talk you into it," I tell her, my eyes flicking to the poster and the date and location of the nearest auditions to us. "But I think you really *should* enter the *Big Dreams* competition this year!"

"*What?* No *way*, Flo!" Mum bursts out laughing, half-relieved that I'm not going to tell her anything awful (yet) and very surprised that I've joined the Dark Side and am trying to persuade her to enter the sort of contest that I know she detests. She says no one on these shows has worked for their fame. That all of them are like performers from Victorian sideshows, there to be prodded, gawped and laughed at.

Plus, of course, despite the beehive and the clothes, the voice and the tattoos, Queenie Brown has zero self-confidence. Why else would she hide herself away in a back-street, old-lady hairdresser when she could work in any big, cutting-edge salon if she wanted?

"But you're *so* good, Mum," I carry on, hoping I sound convincing. "And you *deserve* to be heard."

"I'm sorry, Flo," Mum answers, "but me applying for *Big Dreams* is about as likely as— as—"

Her greeny-brown eyes dart about as she struggles for a simile.

And in that split-second I realize that I might have less time than I thought to work out how to tell her about Crimson Hill coming to town. They might not be playing till the summer, but posters advertising the concert go up sooner than that. And while Mum doesn't read the local paper, she can't miss a colourful poster *screaming* the bad news at her.

"Well, it's as likely us being able to afford that house across the road," she says finally, laughing wryly. "Or – or me getting back together with your dad, even!"

Uh-oh – I just inhaled that whole, biscuit-y mouthful.

What a way to go, I think bleakly, as I choke, splutter and cough. *Death by flapjack. . .*

Sunday 26th February

Luckily, the flapjack didn't kill me.

But talking about death, it turned out it was Mrs Jennings' dying wish that Mum entered the *Big Dreams* competition.

And if one of your best customers says that, what can a talented singing hairdresser do but carry out the wish?

"Look – it's Nathan Reed!" I say, nudging Mum now.

She looks up from her *Big Dreams* information form and gazes across the packed exhibition hall.

The huge, cavernous space is crowded with rows and rows of plastic chairs and hordes and *hordes* of wannabe contestants – plus one famous person, in the shape of Nathan Reed, the very handsome, thirty-something presenter of the show.

"Oh, yes! Look, he's doing one of his roving reports," Mum answers, and we both stare – along with everyone else – at the pretty girl band that he's chatting to, with a cameraman looming in close.

"Maybe he'll come and interview *you*," I suggest to her, feeling a little flip and flutter of excitement in my tummy.

I've never seen anyone famous, ever. It's not as if you get someone like Nathan Reed hanging out in Marigold Parade, popping into the Beanz Café for a muffin, or Armando's for some highlights in his hair.

"Yeah, well, the chances of him interviewing me are pretty small, considering there are a few zillion people to choose from!" Mum smiles.

It's not *quite* a zillion, but there are certainly hundreds – if not thousands – of people waiting to do their stuff in one of the twenty or so audition rooms dotted around.

"You never know, Mu—"

"Queenie? Queenie Brown?" a voice interrupts me.

A girl with a clipboard is glancing around the mobbed hall. Then her eyes settle on Mum and instantly match her unusual, retro name with the unusual, retro-styled person sitting next to me.

"Right," says Mum, smoothing down her now-perfectly-tailored Hawaiian shirt. "Looks like my turn – wish me luck!"

"I wish you a bucketful," I tell her.

I give Mum a hug, but not a kiss, since I don't want to mess up her make-up or the fabric red hibiscus pinned in her hair, to match her shirt. She bought the flower from the 99p Store near the bus station and Olive spent last night snipping off the plastic stem and sewing on a hair clip while Mum rehearsed her song in front of us. (Something from the sixties called "Big Yellow Taxi" by Joni Mitchell.)

As Mum weaves her way through the waiting crowds in her black pumps and turn-up jeans, I don't just watch *her*; I watch everyone else checking her out. Whether it's old ladies in an old-fashioned hairdresser's or a swarm of strangers and their entourages at the *Big Dreams* open auditions, people can't help being mesmerized by her.

SLAP!

My view of Mum instantly vanishes as two hands cover my eyes.

"Guess who?" says a familiar voice.

"Barack Obama?" I suggest, grinning.

"Close; very close," the voice answers with a laugh, as the hands let go.

A scrawny white thirteen-year-old boy who will *never* be President of the United States plonks himself in the seat next to me.

"Well?" I ask Freddie. "How did you get on?"

"Where's Zee?" he asks, infuriatingly ignoring my comment and gazing at the chair next to him with our friend's parka strewn on it.

"Gone to take photos of some of the freaks who are here," I tell him. "She said she saw a bunch of blokes who looked like rugby players all dressed in Babygros."

They'd been practising their harmonies to Justin Bieber's "Baby" (what else?). But Zee said no one was paying them any attention 'cause a bloke dressed as Darth Vader was breakdancing (badly) right beside them.

"Ah, yeah – they were just going into the audition room when I came out," he nods.

"Yeah, well, who cares about the big babies? How did *you* get on?" I push him, tempted to give him a Chinese burn if he doesn't tell me all soon.

Obviously, it wasn't Mrs Jennings' dying wish that *Freddie* enter the *Big Dreams* competition, but once he heard Mum was up for it, he decided it might be a laugh to jump on the bus with us for the hour-long journey to London, *and* the however-many-hours' wait to be seen. (We've been here for ever, but it's been fun watching the amazing and amazingly *awful* contestants all around us.)

"They *adored* me!" Freddie roars, flinging out his arms wide.

I narrow my eyes at him. I don't see him holding

any laminated Silver Ticket . . . and that's how it works. The first bunch of judges aren't anyone famous; just some staff from the *Big Dreams* production team. But if they like you, you get a Silver Ticket, and will be asked to stick around to perform in front of the "real" judges later in the day.

"Nyah," Freddie groans, deflating into the seat and pulling a face. "I didn't get through. I made all the judges laugh, though!"

"Aw, Freddie, I'm sorry," I say, giving his bony shoulders a hug. "But why did they laugh at you? You're really good at 'New York State of Mind'."

He is. Especially when he's doing it properly, and not just hamming it up on a plastic orange chair in the dinner hall. Olive couldn't stop clapping last night when he ran through it, bare-chested, in our living room. (Olive had demanded he hand over his T-shirt with the black and white Union Jack on it so she could fix it – she'd said there was no way he was going to wear it to the audition with the hem hanging down the way it was.)

Freddie pushes his slick of floppy hair off his face, fixes me with an "oops!" look and bites his lip.

"I might have *accidentally* jumped on a chair and pulled my T-shirt off halfway through. . ." he admits.

"You muppet," says Zee, appearing behind us and gently cuffing Freddie around the head with a rolled-up *Big Dreams* info sheet.

"Owwwww!" Freddie roars, theatrically falling off the chair and collapsing on to the floor.

Everyone turns and stares.

I blush furiously, dying to shout out, "He's all right – he does this *all* the time."

Zee sits herself down, faking an uninterested yawn.

"So has Queenie been called already?" she asks, ignoring Freddie as he flails around on the carpet, clutching his head.

"Yes, she just went through a second ago," I tell her.

"Yeah?" says Freddie, stopping dead, his arms and legs in the air like an upturned cockroach. "Wow – she'll blow their minds!"

He may embarrass me in public on a regular basis, but you can't fault Freddie's enthusiasm. *Or* the fact that he really doesn't care about goofing up, being called a dork, acting the fool or blowing his chances at a competition that other (less talented) people would saw their left arm off to be chosen for.

"Hey, have you looked at this *properly*, Flo?" Zee asks, tapping the info sheet.

Why is Zee asking? Of *course* I have. We've been here so long that – in between intense people-watching – I've read it through a bunch of times. I know exactly how the show works.

After this first audition here in London, there will be seven more in main cities around the country.

Starting next month, each city's auditions will be shown, one a week. The best acts from each city will be given Golden Tickets, which means they *may* get selected to go through to the Manor House stage in early summer. They'll get mentored by famous people there, but entrants will be dropped every week, and asked to hand in their Golden Ticket as they leave.

Then in late June and all through July, there will be six live shows, where contestants are voted out left, right and centre.

On the fourth of August – six whole months away – the winner will be chosen and handed a million-pound record contract with the Platinum Music Group.

That's how it all works.

The end.

Or just the *beginning*, really, if you're the winner. . .

"So do you reckon Armando will be OK with Queenie taking time off for the competition?" Zee asks matter-of-factly.

"Well, that's if she gets through," I shrug.

"Come off it – of *course* she will, Flo," Freddie laughs, pushing himself up and coming to sit beside me again. "I mean, if she doesn't, all the Ladies will *kill* her, they're so excited about it. *Especially* Mrs Jennings."

Ah, Mrs Jennings . . . it certainly *looked* like she was dying this time last week, when me and Mum visited her in the hospital. She'd been rushed in the day before with a suspected stroke, and had a drip in her hand and a cold sweat on her forehead when we saw her. She was very confused, calling the male nurse "Armando" and mistaking me for her grandchild (who I knew was a *boy* called Duncan, aged seven).

But she'd recognized Queenie straight away. Like some gorgeous caricature, Mum and her beehive had sashayed up to Mrs Jennings' bed with an armful of flowers and chocolates from just about everyone who lived or worked in Marigold Parade.

Mrs Jennings' eyes had lit up, and the nurse

was pleased; he said it was the first time she'd been lucid all day, even when her family had visited earlier.

He hovered when he saw Mrs Jennings reach for Mum's hand. Listened as Queenie chatted to Mrs Jennings, and Mrs Jennings nodded weakly in response. Stared with amazement as Mrs Jennings struggled to form her first words since she'd arrived on the ward.

"Queenie," she'd whispered weakly. "Say you'll enter that competition on the telly. *Please*. Do it for me – then I can die happy!"

I'd gulped.

The nurse cried.

Mum promised.

But like me with my near-death-by-flapjack moment a week or so ago, Mrs Jennings *didn't* die.

In fact, her "stroke" turned out to be a bad case of food poisoning (she got a lecture from the doctor about eating a month-old chicken drumstick she'd found at the back of her fridge).

But by that time it was too late. Mum couldn't back out; not when Armando's Ladies had heard all about her bedside vow in their visits to the recuperating Mrs Jennings.

But here's the thing: I hadn't thought any further than this audition.

Till Zee mentioned it just now, I hadn't seriously considered Mum getting through to the next round. *And* the round after that.

It wasn't 'cause I doubted how good Mum's voice was. . .

"Look," I begin, "you *know* my mum thinks this whole thing is totally naff. She's only here today because of Mrs Jennings. Even if the judges go nuts for her, she'll just say, 'Thanks, but no tha—'"

Before I get the chance to babble some more about Mum's genuine lack of interest in the show, I'm suddenly aware of rumbling oohs and aahs all around.

"Look – she's got a Silver Ticket!" someone from a nearby huddle of people exclaims.

I look up.

Mum is on her way back, and she is more radiant than ever.

Her dimples say it all – and so does the laminated silver card in her hand.

The judges loved her.

And from the way she's beaming, I suddenly, surprisingly, realize that this *won't* be the end of Queenie's *Big Dreams*.

"Wow . . . she's going to go for it, isn't she?" mutters Freddie, recognizing that light of excitement in Mum's eyes.

I feel a shiver of excitement myself, plus aftershocks of nerves and just a *little* bit of panic.

A big show; a big secret.

If Mum ends up coming home tonight with a *Golden* Ticket, the next few months are going to be, er, *interesting*. . .

MARCH

Saturday 24th March

"Hi!" says a young girl in a sparkly tight top, dark pink shorts and chunky wedge trainers.

The studio audience goes crazy at the sight of last year's *Big Dreams* winner, Celeste Benedict.

"Doesn't she look amazing, ladies and gentlemen?" says Nathan Reed.

The studio audience clap and clap till their hands practically fall off.

"Now how about we take a moment," says Nathan, holding out his hands to plead for quiet, "to look back at little Celeste's journey from schoolgirl to recording star!"

He throws his arm behind him at the giant screens, where Celeste is shown looking cute and goofy in a flouncy party dress at her audition.

The studio audience "Awww!"s and cheers, thrilled to be part of the very first show of this year's *Big Dreams* competition. They'll see clips of all the highlights – and low points – of the London auditions. They'll see the forty or so contestants who were lucky enough to be given Silver Tickets that day. There'll be chats with the judges – a famous dancer, a girl from a TV soap and a bloke who was in a pop band in the 80s – as they reveal the five London acts they chose to receive a Golden Ticket.

Of course, I *know* who one of those acts is. We've had the Golden Ticket on the mantelpiece, tucked behind Mum's unlovely, angular vase, for two months now.

Which means she's had to put up with two months' worth of frenetic excitement and questioning from the Ladies, till now, till the show's finally aired.

It'll take another few weeks – while the various cities' auditions are shown and more Golden Ticket acts are selected – before she'll know whether she'll definitely be chosen to go through to the Manor House stage.

Of course her brain may melt with old-lady hysteria before then.

And *mine* might melt if Freddie keeps bugging me the way he's doing.

We're not in the fancy studio, by the way; this

first show isn't live – it was recorded last night. (Mum was gone all of yesterday, so at the end of all the clips, she could perform her "Big Yellow Taxi" song on the stage, while the other Golden Ticket-ers did *their* performances.)

Nope, where I am is squashed on the sofa at home between a shoal of koi carp and a couple of cheerleader pom-poms.

"Quit it!" I say to Freddie, pushing one of the pom-poms out of my face.

"Oh, don't be such a spoilsport, Flo," grumbles Olive, from the comfort of one of the two armchairs. Like I say, she's not keen on having males in our family (thanks to previous experience), but she's very happy to have male friends in the living room. *Our* living room, anyway, me and Mum's.

"Where's Queenie gone?" asks Wolfie, looking over the back of the sofa in search of Mum, who's scarpered to the kitchen, mumbling about making more tea.

Now that Wolfie's turned around, I'm no longer hemmed in by the koi carp that cover his left arm. I leap up and grab the empty bowls from the coffee table, with a view to refilling them with crisps while the Celeste section is on.

"Y'know, that red really goes with your eyes," I tell Freddie as I head off, nodding my head to the ketchup-coloured pom-poms that he borrowed from the Lost and Found box under the Beanz Café counter.

(He's made up a cheerleader chant to shout out every time we see Mum on the screen. It's basically just "QueenEEE! QueenEEE! QueenEEE!")

"*Very* funny," he retorts. "Now hurry and bring us more snacks, wench!"

I bend away so I miss the whack of pom-pom he aims at my bottom.

BUZZZZ!

"I'll get it," I say, since I'm up and only a few footsteps away from the intercom on the wall.

Without asking who it is, I press the button that automatically unlocks the downstairs front door and yank the flat door open with my free hand.

"Yoo-hoo!" Angie Rossi calls as she pads up the stairs. "Room for two little ones?"

"Of course – we've reserved two seats for you in the back, madame," I tell Freddie's mum, whose lighter footsteps are followed by the heavier ones of Mario, Freddie's dad. I can smell them as well as hear them; a fresh scent of shampoo and soap.

Saturday's always their busiest day, and they have to stay late cleaning up, followed by showers to wash away the clinging smells of bacon, chips and custard.

"Haven't missed our stars yet, have we?" says Angie, as she steps in the flat. "We had the TV on at the shop and then at ours and one of us kept checking it."

"Nope; the first part's just been introducing the judges and recapping on last year's show," I assure them, closing the door and letting Angie and Mario find their own way in. Which isn't hard, since their flat next door is identical to ours.

With the guests sorted, I peek into the kitchen – but there's no sign of Mum. Bathroom? Nope, the door's open. Her bedroom?

Yes, there she is, staring out at the street below. Her shoulder is holding back the trailing drape of fine Indian silk (£1.50, RSPCA charity shop) covering the window.

"The auditions section must be starting soon," I tell her, wondering why she's here, like this, when there's a room full of people next door. "Are you OK?"

"I'm just feeling a little nervous, that's all," she

says, the dimples in her cheeks appearing and disappearing as her smile wavers. "It's been a long time since I sang in public."

I walk over to her, glancing at my watch. "Yeah, a *really* long time. Has it been more than two hours already since the hairdresser's shut?"

Mum smiles more genuinely at my teasing. But I'm unsettled to notice her nervous tic's making an appearance. Whenever she's wobbly she rubs the thumb of her right hand around (and around) the black lily on the inside of her left wrist.

"I don't mean in front of you and the Ladies and everyone," Mum continues, putting her forehead on the cool glass of the windowpane. "It's just the idea that *everyone's* watching the show, right now, and they'll see me in the clips, and then on stage at the end."

I join her and gaze down into the street too. Across in the sheltered houses with their frilly net curtains, I can make out the fuzzy, coloured glow of screen after TV screen, all tuned into *Big Dreams*. Maureen, Nora, Mrs Jennings, Mrs Georgiou and the others.

Of course, the Ladies aren't the only ones who'll be glued to the telly tonight: Zee and her family two doors up; Armando in his nice house by the tennis courts (which sadly, he has to share with Valerie and Roxanne, since Valerie's marriage broke up); Bernard and Philip from the dry-cleaner's in their bachelor pad overlooking the river; very probably the students above the accountants and the accountant guy himself, wherever he calls home. *All* of Marigold Parade will be watching, one way or another, one place or another.

Then there's everyone at school, though they'll be mainly tuning in to catch a glimpse of Freddie, of course.

And I'm not even thinking about the audience of millions, all around the country. . .

"Hurry up," yells a member of the audience in our living room. "The audition part is starting!"

"Right," says Mum, straightening herself up and leading the way back to the others.

I hope she doesn't suddenly develop the ability to read minds.

'Cause I'm now wondering if there's a chance someone *else* might be watching.

I mean, I know they're busy, famous, international rock stars, but Crimson Hill and their crew are human too, aren't they? Maybe they're backstage somewhere in the UK right now, whiling away the time till they perform by checking out the programme that *everyone's* hooked on.

How totally weird to think that any minute now, my dad could be setting eyes on my mother for the first time in eleven years.

"Oi, wench! Where's the popcorn?" I hear Freddie shout to me.

The thought of food suddenly makes me feel a little sick.

Probably because the secret Something is tightening into a hard, huge knot in my tummy. . .

Monday 26th March

"Amazing! AMAZING! A-M-A-Z-I-N-G!!"

I'm blinking at the avalanche of enthusiasm coming from Polly Clarke.

Though out of the corner of my eye,.I can see that our bus is coming.

"Omigod, my whole family were like, 'You KNOW that woman?'" adds Heidi. "And I'm screaming, 'Yeah, I *do*. She's my friend Flo's mum!'"

Wow, this has been going on all day: pupils,

teachers, dinner ladies . . . they've all been prattling about Mum and the *Big Dreams* auditions show on Saturday night.

Freddie's been getting it too, of course. Our head teacher, Mrs Holmes, even made him stand up and take a bow at assembly. (I just waved shyly when she mentioned my mum.)

Even though he did it purely for laughs and looked a total, lovable numpty on telly, it's still raised his status to celeb at school. He even did a repeat performance at break time. He got as far as taking his tie off and waving it round his head, but thankfully the bell went before he had the chance to go bare-chested again. . .

"C'mon, Flo – it's here," says Zee, tugging me on to the No. 34.

"And don't forget, girls!" Freddie shouts to Polly and Heidi as he follows us on. "I'll sign an autograph for you anytime, with a free kiss thrown in. All you have to do is ask!"

I spot Polly and Heidi rolling their eyes as we flash our passes at the driver and find ourselves a seat.

"Ahem."

That's Zee doing a fake cough. (Actually, she looks a lot like the Asian equivalent of a Charlotte Brontë consumptive heroine – skinny, pretty, with huge sad eyes – so the coughing kind of suits her, weirdly.)

"Yes?" I say, knowing she wants a response.

"Heidi told her family that she knows your mum. Since when?" she asks bluntly.

"Since she met her for two seconds in the café in Pear Tree Avenue in the half-term holidays," I answer, with a wry smile.

"Hmm, that's a *deep* friendship, for sure," Zee nods sagely.

It *is* funny when you think about it, isn't it? One minute you're not too interesting, then next – after your mother's got a little sniff of fame – it's like you've got this glow of specialness about you.

I'm kind of enjoying it, if I'm honest. But I'm not sure I'll say so to Zee – I might get a lecture about how fake it all is.

"So Queenie's going through with it, then?" Freddie asks. "She's not having second thoughts?"

"Nope – she's still up for it," I reply. I'm only just getting used to the fact that Mum's changed from hating the very idea of talent shows to being a willing participant. "She's excited. She says she hadn't realized how good it would make her feel about herself."

I think of the newish dice tattoo – the one Wolfie

said she had done because she was feeling fed-up. Maybe the number six had brought her luck after all. . .

"Whoops!" cried Zee.

"What?" I say, startled after drifting off in my own thoughts for a second there.

Have we missed our stop? No – we're now idling near the bus station, letting passengers off. Our stop's next.

"Look over there, Flo. . ."

Zee is pointing to a long-empty shop. Its huge window's now become an unofficial advertising site for fly-posters, and in amongst the overlapping ads for clubs and DJ events, there's an extra-large one featuring a mulberry pink mountain and the distinctive "Crimson Hill" logo.

So it's happening.

"I'm going to *have* to tell her," I mutter, the knot in my stomach twisting ever tighter, like it does every time I think of Dad.

"Well, that IS what we've been telling you to do for. . ." Zee looks at her watch ". . .the last couple of *months*, Flo."

"C'mon, it's us next," says Freddie, getting to his feet and pressing the bell.

With Zee's well-meaning sarcasm ringing in my ears, I follow my friends down the stairs and get off at the stop on Grey Street.

Once we cross the crazy-busy four lanes of traffic and land safely at Marigold Parade, I'm half expecting Zee to carry on lecturing me about my uselessness, but it doesn't happen.

Instead, she's staring at the small crowd outside Hair By Armando.

So am I.

So is Freddie.

"Hi!" bellows Wolfie, who's leaning against a lamp post, observing the commotion.

"What's going on?" I ask.

I'm not particularly tall and can't see over the huddle of people around the entrance of the hairdresser's.

"The local newspaper are here," explains Wolfie, who's big as it is, and bigger still in his chunky biker boots. "Here, Flo."

He gets down on one knee and holds out a hand to me.

For a horrible second it's as if he's about to propose.

"Come on then!" Wolfie says, nodding at his knee, and I realize he's offering me a step up to see what's going on, rather than a ring and a lifetime of wedded bliss.

Giggling, I take his hand and stand on his denimed knee.

"What can you see?" asks Zee.

"Your mum and dad," I tell her, spotting Mr and Mrs Chowdri and baby Roo amongst a gaggle of Armando's Ladies. "Yours too, Freddie."

Olive, Bernard and Philip from the dry-cleaner's; they're in the mini-crowd too. And a bloke in a shirt and tie who's the never-much-seen accountant who's got his office next to Wolfie's.

"Yeah, but what's going on?" Freddie asks, as he dumps his school bag and starts to climb up the lamp post.

"The *Herald*'s interviewing Queenie about her TV appearance," Wolfie explains, while I gawp at Mum.

She's leaning in the doorway of the salon, looking cute with a vintage paisley scarf tied around her dark pile of hair, her bright red smile at full beam and a hairbrush in her hand. Armando, in his shirt, tie and grey trousers is standing beside her, chest out.

"I'm so proud of her!" he's bellowing to the journalist with her recorder and the crowd in general. "Queenie is . . . is like a daughter to me!"

Well, that comment went down well with everyone, by the sound of the clapping and cheering.

Except for the two sour faces I can see through the plate-glass window. And it's not just Valerie and Roxanne who didn't like that comment; anyone would guess that Olive was currently sucking a lemon.

I hope Mum doesn't notice. She's always smiley and happy, but right now there's some extra, added shininess about her that I've never really seen before.

I don't want anyone to spoil this time for her.

Then again, *I* might just be about to do that myself.

It's weeks overdue, but it's time to tell Mum about the Something.

This is one secret that *needs* to spill, before the knot in my stomach tightens so much it splits me in two. . .

APRIL

Wednesday 11th April

The story of Mum and Dad.

I guess it's the usual story of boy meets girl: they fall in love, promise to be together for ever, get tattoos half an hour after a huge fight to show they're still mad about each other (tiny pony for her, *Queenie Forever* for him), girl has baby, boy gets job with a band, boy tours the world, boy never comes back.

OK, maybe it's *not* so usual.

But it's my family's story and it's swirling around in my head right now, same as Mum's thumb is swirling around on her black lily.

I reach across the table and put my hand on her wrist.

"What are you thinking about?" I ask her.

I hope she doesn't ask me the same question back.

Because all that's in my head is the fact that I have to tell her about Dad coming to town.

Now.

Well, in the next few minutes.

Or at least, before we leave the Woodlands Café. I've promised myself, and I've promised Zee and Freddie I'll do it too.

Actually, Zee has threatened to unfriend me on Facebook and in real life if I don't sort this out. (I know she wouldn't, but I appreciate her dark threats, 'cause I know she just wants me to do the right thing.)

Freddie had threatened never to give me free chips from the caff ever again. (That's almost as serious as Zee's threat in my book.)

"What am I thinking about?" Mum smiles, answering my question with a question. "Oh, y'know . . . no surprises – I'm just a bit nervous about the visit."

We've come to the Pear Tree Avenue charity shops on a mission this afternoon: sometime soon, the *Big Dreams* team will be coming to see her (film her!), and she wants to look her best. Because it's the Easter holidays and Mum's half day, we hiked it over here, determined to scour every rack for something that Olive could transform into an amazing outfit. In the end, Mum blew all her tips money, plus a bit extra, on three bags full of possibilities.

So far – packed in our little living room with our friends and neighbours – we've watched the audition shows for London, Birmingham and Glasgow. There's plenty more to come: Cardiff this coming Saturday, followed by Bristol, Belfast, Manchester and Newcastle.

But even before those shows have been aired, the "You're in" or "You're out" visits from Nathan Reed will be happening for contestants like Mum, to be shown at a future date. . .

I don't know about her, but I'm pretty nervous at the idea of someone off the telly sitting in our living room, cameras and lights blazing, while they tell Mum whether or not she's got a place at the Manor House.

Still, I'm *twice* as nervous about sitting here alone with Mum right now.

I pick a crumb off the huge "half" a muffin in front of me and try to eat it, but it sticks in my throat, perched on the words that are lodged there.

"So, no 'Sold' sign on our new home yet, eh, Flo?" Mum smiles, nodding her head towards the white Regency house across the road.

"Mmm," I mumble.

"Hey, maybe I'll win the *Big Dreams* competition, get offered the million-pound record contract, and we could buy it?" she jokes.

"Mmm," I mumble again, with what I hope looks even *slightly* like a smile on my face.

"And you know, this competition; I'm not just in this for myself, Flo. I'm doing it for all of us. Me, you and Olive," says Mum, suddenly sounding earnest. "If by some amazing piece of luck I do well, it could change *everything*. Maybe we could move to a nicer area; eat in places like this all the time. Olive could afford to retire at last. I can buy you clothes that *aren't* out of the Cancer Research Shop. Life could be – well, roses and cherries and sugar sprinkles on top!"

I just smile, knowing that's all just dreams and fluff. Like I say, I sometimes feel more of a grown-up than Mum, and right now I know that her voice is amazing, but I also know that there are always a *ton* of amazing people on shows like *Big Dreams,* and only one or two ever actually have a showbiz career afterwards.

"But hey, everything's been all about *me* lately," Mum says, changing the subject. "Are you OK?

You've been a bit quiet, babe. What's going on in World of Flo?"

Queenie might not look or sometimes act like the average parent, but it seems she still has a standard-fit mother's intuition.

So.

This is my moment.

This is when I spit it out (probably with a crumb of muffin, knowing me).

"Listen, Mum, I—"

There's a gust of wind and a giggle of voices as the door opens.

"Oh, hi, Flo – and Mrs Brown!" Polly and Heidi practically say in unison.

They're not with the guitar boy this time; they're with a couple of girls I've never seen before. But from their uniform I can tell the girls go to Lady Margaret's, the nearby private school. And I can tell from their shocked expressions that they've recognized Mum. If they were in any doubt, she confirms it straight away.

"*Please* call me Queenie. Mrs Brown makes me sound like my mother."

Though, of course, technically, Gran is actually a "Miss". Miss Olive Brown, same as Mum is

Miss Queenie Rae Brown. We're the three Miss Browns. (But that's another story.)

"Mrs Brown – I mean, *Queenie*," babbles one of the girls I don't know. "I've watched every audition show so far and I'm not kidding; you are *so* the best."

"This is my friend Gabrielle," Polly butts in with an introduction as Mum smiles and flashes her dimples.

"And I'm Alexa," says the other girl.

They both have long, perfectly smooth bouncy hair, just like Polly and Heidi. I run a hand self-consciously over my bob. My fine, flyaway, shoulder-length, growing-out, messy bob.

"I hope you get through to the Manor House stage," says Heidi. "When do you find out?"

"Well, pretty soon," Mum replies. "But it won't go out on the telly for a while, so whichever way it goes, I'll have to keep it a secret."

I'm feeling a bit left out of this conversation. All eyes are on Mum. I might as well go to the loo right now 'cause no one will notice if I'm not h—

"Hey, Flo," Polly suddenly says. "We're all going off to Centre Parcs with our parents this weekend."

Well, thanks for sharing that/showing off, I think

to myself, trying to keep an interested smile on my face.

"But the *next* Saturday we're having a bit of a *Big Dreams* party round at Alexa's, to watch the Bristol auditions. Do you want to come?"

"Yes, *please* come," says the girl who's Alexa. "It's only over there – that white house with the 'For Sale' sign. We're trying to move to one of the big houses by the park."

Clunk.

That's the sound of a chunk of my life slotting into place.

I'm being invited to hang out with the Forest Park girls, in the house of our dreams?! Far away from dull little Marigold Parade?

Sounds like fun, fun, fun – but then I think of Mum and home.

Mum, who needs looking after.

"Well, thanks, but I usually watch it with. . ."

"Don't be silly, Flo," says Mum, guessing that I'm trying to back out for *her* sake. "You have fun with your friends. I'll watch it with your gran and Wolfie and everyone."

I see the girls all twitch, obviously dying to know who "Wolfie" is. I don't suppose there're too many

Wolfies at Lady Margaret's School For Girls, and certainly not any stubbly-chinned ones with koi carp on their arms that inflate when they flex their muscles.

A millisecond before I reply, I think of Freddie – but he won't care. He doesn't care about anything, except acting like a baboon. And Zee doesn't count – Saturday nights are family-nights-in for her, 'cause of her grandparents and aunties and uncles all piling round.

"Thanks, I'd like that," I say to Alexa, and Polly too.

"Great. So a week on Saturday, around seven p.m., then?" Polly says, checking with Alexa that it sounds about right.

"Sure," I nod, still stunned at my invite.

"Well, see you then," Polly says with a wave, as they head towards a table at the back.

I turn to Mum and we're exchanging wide-eyed, who'd-have-thought-it stares when Polly bounds back into view.

"Hey – just thinking, Flo," she says. "Do you like Crimson Hill?"

I open and close my mouth like a drowning goldfish. Polly seems to mistake the reason behind my gargly choking face.

"Yeah, I mean, I *know* they're kind of a dad band," she carries on, not realizing how that sounds to me, on *two* levels. "But they are *legends* and everything and it's unbelievable that they're playing in a little town like ours. Anyway, a bunch of us are going, and there's a spare ticket – if you fancy it?"

Now Polly mistakes my stunned silence for thought, I reckon, rather than sheer unadulterated *panic*.

"Well, think it over and let me know when we're back at school, yeah?"

With a smile Polly's gone.

I'm still facing where she was, too horrified to turn around and look at Mum.

Then I feel her hand on mine.

"I'm sorry, Flo," she says. "I've known Crimson Hill were coming for a while, but I didn't know how to tell you!"

Huh?

"You *knew*?" I squeak, spinning my head around so quick I feel dizzy. "Since when?"

"Oh, I think it was in the *Herald* back in January sometime. Your gran saw the article and told me about it. She reckons it was your dad who must've persuaded the band to play the Astoria – he always loved that venue. We used to go there together back when . . . well, a long time ago."

Mum's black-winged eyes blink nervously, waiting for me to react to the shock news that my dad will be in town.

"The thing is, I saw the same article," I admit to her. "But I didn't know how to tell *you*. Zee and Freddie have been nagging me about it for *weeks* now."

"No way! *Really?* Well, your gran's been going crazy at *me*: 'When are you going to tell Flo? When? *Hmm?*'"

She puts her hands on her hips and does a mean impersonation of Olive, and I can't help but laugh. She joins in, probably as relieved as I am that our shared secret is out.

And then slowly, our sniggers stop.

It's time to ask each other some uncomfortable questions, I guess.

"How do you feel about it, Flo?" Mum starts.

"I – I don't know," I answer, wondering how to describe the hard, tight knot I've been walking around with for so long. But in the meantime, I can ask her *my* question. "Mum . . . what'll happen?"

I want *her* to be the adult for once, to have a perfect answer.

But as she reaches across to hug me, I see the tiny dice on her arm – the tattoo she got when she felt down.

It suddenly hits me; it's so obvious! At the time Mum had it done, she'd felt down *because she'd just heard the news about Dad*.

"I wish I knew, Flo," Mum says softly and sadly, as clueless as me. . .

Saturday 21st April

Once upon a time, Olive had a life a lot more colourful than the inside of our flat.

Once upon a time, she was the wardrobe mistress for a snooty supper club in the West End of London. Famous celebs of the time came in their smart suits and fancy frocks to eat, laugh and chat, to listen to bands and crooning singers, to watch the dancing girls. And it was Olive's job to dress the dancers, making sure their glittery corsets, feathery headdresses and elbow-length satin gloves were suitably spangled and sequinned.

"Must have been amazing," I said to her, when I was old enough to understand this bit of her history.

"Amazingly *hard work*," she'd answered dismissively, brushing aside my hopes of seeing a photo or two from her heyday. She brushed aside any questions about her husband-of-five-minutes too. "I don't want to waste my breath talking about him," she'd said bluntly. ("They met at the club, but she divorced him quickly and went back to her maiden name," Mum explained, filling in a gap. "So it's *her* surname I ended up with, not my father's.")

And now here was Olive, sitting in the window of Bernard and Philip's shop, hunched over her latest sewing project.

And here *I* was, asking her for *another* story. Just not one about *her*.

"Tell me again," I beg my gran.

The dry-cleaner's is officially closed for the day, and with smiley owners Bernard and Philip long gone to their home and their pet labradoodle, I'm perched cross-legged on the long counter.

"What's to tell? You've heard it all before," says my gran, concentrating on the bottle-green satin dress that she's turning into an off-the-shoulder top for Mum's next appearance on *Big Dreams*. (The visit, happening sometime in the next couple of weeks, the production team have promised Mum.)

Behind Olive is a corkboard with all her orders on it, instructions on hems that need sewing, rips that need stitching, zips that need to be replaced. But pride of place on there at the moment is the article from the *Herald*, with Mum standing in the doorway of Armando's, holding a hairbrush as if it's a microphone. It's a cheesy pose which she was made to do, but she still looks gorgeous. I notice Olive has cut off the headline that went with it.

("'Small-Time Hairdresser Has Big Dreams'?" Olive had read out aloud when she first saw it. "The cheek of them – my Queenie's not 'small-time'!")

"It's been forever since I've heard the story," I remind my gran, "and I'm scared I've forgotten it, or I'm remembering it wrong. And I *need* to know, especially now."

"There's nothing different about 'now', Flo," says Olive, looking up sharply from her sewing. "He may be coming back here with that band, but you won't see him. He'll come, do his show, and then he'll be back on the tour coach or whatever you call it. So don't go expecting more. You *or* your mother."

I'd hoped that now the secret Mum and I had been keeping from each other was out there, I could talk to Olive about it. But who was I kidding? Her hatred for my dad ran pretty deep.

"Look, I'm not expecting him to turn up with armfuls of flowers and sorries after eleven years. I'm just asking if you'll tell me again how they got together," I say, trying to sound calm, even if I'm getting riled with her. The trouble is, if you lose your temper with Olive, she'll just purse her lips and become even *more* immovable than ever.

"Right," says Olive, with a weary sigh. "Your mum had a crush on your dad when *she* was at college and *he* played guitar in some café or bar or other."

She runs her needle fast and hard over the material under her hands, as if she's imagining doing the same thing to my dad's head.

"Anyway, they met *properly* when she was twenty-two and was working in the salon in the high street; she styled his *quiff* for him."

With a sour face, Olive puts her hands to her head and mimics Dad's upright rockabilly hairdo.

"And?" I push her.

"And Queenie fell in love with him, and his silly quiff," she sighs again.

"She'd sing while he played his guitar, wouldn't she?" I remember this, from some long-ago conversation.

"Hmm. So they muddled along for a few years together, madly in love, then falling out and getting back together. He always promised they'd go to Las Vegas and get married in some Elvis chapel or some nonsense. But that never happened, of course. What happened was *you* came along, and off your dad went, into thin air."

"But he didn't go as *soon* as I was born," I point out. "And he *did* stay in touch for a while after he left."

I was two when he said oops, he was going on a year-long world tour with Crimson Hill. Oh, and that he thought "it wasn't working" with him and Mum. After that, he sent cards for our birthdays and Christmases for a few years. And postcards too . . . like the one from New York that I keep in the box under my bed. But then the cards trailed off, till they stopped altogether.

Chunks of money – his version of child support, I suppose – appear once in a blue moon in Queenie's bank account.

And that's it.

All there is to show that my dad's alive and out there in the world somewhere.

"What's the difference?" says Olive. "Your dad left.

End of story. Now don't go bothering your mother with any questions like these; she doesn't need to be thinking about *him* when she's got the chance to concentrate on herself for once."

Of *course* I wasn't going to ask Mum about it; that was the reason I'd come to talk to Olive. Since our moment in the Woodlands Café a week or so ago, me and Mum hadn't mentioned the "D" word again to each other. Like Mum had said at the time, we had no idea if Dad planned to get in touch, or be as silent and distant as ever, so what was the point in worrying and wondering ab—

"Check it out!"

With a clatter of the door and a flap of the "Sorry we're closed" sign, Freddie barges in, flapping a newspaper about, with Zee flitting in behind him.

"Mr Chowdri just noticed it," Freddie says in a mad rush, spreading the newspaper flat beside me on the counter.

"What's the matter?" asks Olive with a frown, scuttling up from behind her sewing machine.

"Page five of the *Mirror* – *that's* what's the matter," Zee explains, without making sense.

We look.

We gawp.

Uncomfortable shivers ripple up and down my back.

An hour later, I'm with a different set of someones, all looking, all gawping.

I'm in the beautiful Regency house in Pear Tree Avenue. We're supposed to be watching the *Big Dreams* audition show from Bristol on the living room's giant flat-screen TV, but no one's paying it any attention.

With their long, perfect hair falling forward, Polly, Heidi, Alexa and Gabrielle study the photos in the national newspaper, spread out on the glass-topped coffee table.

National newspaper, I repeat silently to myself, which means that, *nationwide*, strangers will have stared and gossiped over those photos of "Charity Chic Singer" Queenie Brown "and her daughter" browsing the second-hand clothes in the Forest Park Cancer Research shop in the Easter holidays.

"Wow, Flo, you're famous!" says Polly.

First, it was the local newspaper that flagged up the fact that my dad would be in town; now a national one had spied on me and Mum.

I don't know about being famous, but reading

about my life in black and white feels weird, and not at all wonderful.

"Hey, to think: if the paparazzi had stuck around for a few minutes longer," Heidi adds, "they might have taken photos of *us* talking to you and your mum in the café, Flo."

Alexa's house is as fantastic inside as out – filled with expensive modern and antique furniture, unlike our flat, full of sale stuff from IKEA and junk shop finds. But special as this house is and as lovely as these girls are being to me, I'm not sure I'm in the right mood to enjoy myself.

I mean, I do *want* to have fun . . . to have fun and forget Mum's face going whiter-than-white earlier when she realized we'd been stalked that day by an unseen photographer.

But all I keep thinking about is how this article makes me look to Polly and everyone. How do I explain that just because me and Mum are looking at second-hand clothes, it doesn't mean we're poor; it's just that we're not rich? And that we're certainly not desperate; we *love* finding hidden treasure. . .

"Have you noticed that you're just mentioned as '*hot favourite Queenie's teenage daughter*'?" Alexa points out now.

"You know what *that* means," comes a boy's voice.

"What?" Alexa asks her twin brother, who hasn't said a word up till now.

He's called Marley. He's the boy I saw weeks ago in the café with Polly and Heidi; the one with the guitar thrown across his back. He's strumming it now, drowning out the acts on the TV that no one's watching, they're so fascinated by the newspaper spread out on the floor. He seems a little bored, I think. And I guess I think that because he's said nothing directly to me, or anyone else, since I arrived.

"They're going to snoop around and find out more about you."

Five girls turn to stare at Marley, but Marley just stares at me, with eyes just a paler, greyer shade of Freddie's.

"What do you mean?" I ask him.

He pushes up the long sleeves of his faded blue granddad T-shirt, and from his arms I can tell he's slim, but not as sinewy as Freddie.

The eyes, the build, the floppy hair; Marley's like a better looking, better fed version of my best friend. *And* he can play guitar. (Freddie can just play the fool.)

"Look, they're not going to let it go with just a few photos. Not if your mum carries on doing well in the competition," he says. "They'll want to know your name, your favourite subject at school, if you have a boyfriend. Basically, you'd better get used to it."

Wow, thanks for nothing, I think. He might remind me of my best friend in some ways, but he's not like my funny, sweet best mate at *all*, really.

"Listen, I'm not really feeling that great," I tell Polly and the other girls. "I think I'm just going to go."

They "aww" and seem genuinely disappointed.

Marley strums his guitar and blinks his long-lashed eyes at me.

I have absolutely *no* idea what he's thinking.

Freak. . .

MAY

Friday 4th May

"Are you OK, Queenie?"

That's Nathan Reed talking.

But he's not on a TV screen now; it's 4:30 p.m. on Friday afternoon and he's here in *Marigold Parade*.

I *know*! How exciting is that?

Nathan is perched on a chair in the middle of Hair By Armando, to be precise. Flanked by cameras and sound recordists and other TV people, if you want to be even *more* precise.

He's looking straight at my mum, who's been told to perch on one of Armando's swivelly chairs. The director has told us where we all need to go, and so me and Olive are either side of Mum, with Armando told to cuddle up to my gran (uh-oh) and Valerie and Roxanne told to stand beside me, as if they're a caring auntie and grown-up cousin or something.

Beyond us are a gaggle of Ladies, all beaming and clucking, like happy, white-haired hens.

And beyond *them* – just out of camera range – are a bunch of people who *really* matter. Wolfie, Freddie and Zee; Angie and Mario Rossi; Mr and Mrs Chowdri and Rohan (Roo for short); Bernard and Philip.

Oh, and look: even Ben, Kenzo and Tim – the three students currently living above the accountant's shop – are here, along with Mr Gregory, the accountant guy himself. Even HE'S been drawn away from his facts and figures to see Queenie Brown being told the glad or sad news.

"I'm fine, thanks, Nathan," says Mum, looking a tiny bit nervous but with her voice steady and sweet.

Alongside her trademark baggy jeans and flat pumps, she's wearing her green silk top, which now sits off her pale shoulders. The puff sleeve hides her new dice, but the tumble of roses are on show down her left arm, and the shooting star (for me) is just visible above her heart.

"Then Queenie – it's time to tell you the news. . ." Nathan intones slowly.

We all wait.

Nathan says nothing.

We all wait some more.

Nathan says nothing.

I know it's for dramatic effect (I've seen enough of these programmes) but it really is quite irritating, actually.

And out of the corner of my eye I can make out Olive's fingers, drumming on the back of Mum's chair.

Honestly, the TV producers are doing something pretty risky here. If Nathan doesn't spill the news in the next half a second, she's likely to blow the whole thing by barking, "Oh, for goodness' sake – just spit it out!"

"QUEENIE RAE BROWN – YOU'RE *THROUGH* TO THE MANOR HOUSE!" Nathan suddenly roars, punching the air and rushing to scoop Mum up from her seat.

We're all roaring, all hugging.

It's brilliant news. The best *ever*.

And from the mouth of *an actual TV celebrity*.

But as the chaos of cheers continues, I notice a couple of things I don't like.

I don't like the way Nathan Reed is holding Mum tight, spinning her round and round and sort of *nuzzling* her neck.

I don't like the way Wolfie is glowering at Nathan Reed.

Also, I don't like it that Marley might be right. A couple of weeks ago at his and Alexa's house, he warned me that the press attention would get worse. So far I'd been on high alert, but had seen no photographers and zero journalists. But after this, it could – *would?* – all change. After all, very soon, my mum will be installed in some swanky, vast mansion in London, her every move watched by millions.

And of course something *else* is happening in the not-too-distant future.

I've been trying not to think about it – about *him* – too much, but as the date of the Crimson Hill gig crawls ever closer, I think I'm starting to unravel around the edges.

"Everything's coming up roses, eh, Flo?" says Freddie's mum Angie, coming over and giving my shoulders a squeeze.

I give her a watery smile, hoping *she's* right, and the current knot of dread in my tummy is wrong. . .

It's party time, Marigold Parade style (so don't go expecting too much).

"Can I tempt you?" I say, holding out a paper plate to two Ladies with hair puffy as white candyfloss.

"Ooh, don't mind if I do, Flo my love," says Maureen, helping herself to an egg mayonnaise sandwich with the crusts cut off. "Now while you're here, can you explain to Lilian why this is all hush-hush? She's got herself in an awful muddle!"

Lilian nods. "I watched *Big Dreams* last night, expecting to see the film of us all in Armando's, with that Nathan chappie – but it was just a load of people from Manchester singing and dancing and making fools of themselves on stage."

I watched that myself last night, round at Alexa's, of course. It was the second last of the audition shows – Newcastle next week wraps up this stage of the competition.

Lots of the Ladies were getting muddled and impatient. To them it had seemed forever ago that Mum went to the London audition, and they were desperate to see her on screen again.

"Well, Nathan Reed and his team have to work their way around the country, visiting *lots* of contestants," I tell Lilian. "And once all those visits are done, they'll be compiled and it'll be on the telly. The week after next, actually."

Did that make sense? Lilian's wrinkling her nose a little, struggling to take the programme scheduling on-board.

"And till then, it's a case of shh!" Maureen adds, dramatically tapping a finger to her mouth. "Those TV people want to keep 'who's-in, who's out' as a surprise, don't they, Flo, dear?"

"They certainly do," I reply.

Copying Maureen, I put my own finger to my mouth, which could look a little strange to anyone entering a party.

Like Mrs Jennings and Mrs Georgiou just have.

"Ooh, this is *lovely*!" Mrs Jennings croons as they step into the long-empty shop between the Chowdris' Newsagent and D.B. Gregory Accountants.

At the same time, just a few steps away, someone's looking round the vacant space with less forgiving eyes. It's funny how people can look at exactly the same thing and see something completely different.

"This is the *pits*," Valerie grumbles to Roxanne

as they stare at the clusters of half-inflated balloons pinned on to the damp walls.

Well, yes, I guess you *can* tell that the shop's been empty a long time. The wallpaper looks like it's trying to roll itself away from the plaster, as if it's allergic to it. The drawing pins holding the balloons up are probably doing a good job of uniting the paper and the wall.

But then Armando – who is the landlord of this place – has turned it into a mini party space at amazingly short notice, so the whole of Marigold Parade can celebrate Queenie Rae Brown making it through to the next round of the *Big Dreams* competition.

Well, when I say the "whole" of Marigold Parade, I don't count the mother-and-daughter Ugly Sisters.

"Yeah, it's *definitely* the pits," Roxanne agrees with her mum, meanly prodding a balloon with her long, cerise plastic nail.

They have their backs to us, so they don't spot Olive bearing down on them.

Uh-oh.

"I didn't see either of *you* two in here this morning, offering to help Armando," Olive growls.

"Me and Mum go to spinning class at our

gym on Sunday mornings," Roxanne replies tartly. "Anyway, Granddad didn't ask."

"I *bet* he didn't," says Olive, turning away to offer snacks to some of the other partygoers. "Lazy so-and-sos. . . ."

Roxanne pulls a face behind Olive's back, I notice as I hurry after Olive.

"I didn't know you cared!" I whisper in my gran's ear.

"About what, dear?" she replies, frowning as Ben, Kenzo and Tim – the three students from the flat next door – help themselves to a handful of sausage rolls each. She gives them a slap on the hand and they guiltily release their fistfuls of food.

"Sticking up for Armando, I mean!" I whisper some more, so he doesn't hear me, though I can see him on the far side of the room, chatting with Nora and Wolfie (hope Wolfie isn't trying to persuade them to get matching Celtic armband tattoos or something).

"Oh, that old fool," Olive shrugs off my comment. "Don't care about *him* . . . just care about reminding those selfish women that other people work hard and don't have things handed to them on a plate."

I guess she's talking about that big house by

the tennis courts that Roxanne and Valerie have "temporarily" shared with Armando for the last three years, since Roxanne's mum and dad split up. Me, Mum and Olive got invited around there last year for Christmas drinks but it wasn't much fun. Valerie and Roxanne spent all their time nagging Armando till it annoyed Olive so much she pretended she had sciatica and demanded we leave.

I guess that makes my gran quite a fair – if grumpy – person.

Suddenly, I hear a drum roll – of sorts. Well, it's actually Freddie, hammering some salad servers on the wall to get everyone's attention.

"Listen, everyone!" Mum calls out, her beehive, her red-lipped smile, her dimples like a beacon lighting up the room.

No one listens; all the assembled Ladies break into a burst of "For she's a jolly good fellow!" It's sweet, and I would join in, only I'm trying to silence the mobile that's started beeping in my pocket.

"Please! *Don't!* You're embarrassing me!" I hear Mum say with a laugh in her voice, as people finally quieten down (and as I manoeuvre my phone out of my too-tight jeans pocket). "Honestly,

I'm terrible at speeches. So all I want to say is a huge thanks to Armando for organizing this, thank you all for supporting me, and arghh – I don't know *how* I'm going to be away from my baby girl for so long!"

It takes a second and a lot of people staring till I realize she's talking about *me*.

"Come here, you. . ." Mum says, holding out her arms.

And next thing I'm being cuddled tight, to the accompanying sounds of many "Awwww!"s.

But what would Mum think if she knew about the message I'd just read?

"Remember – that ticket for Crimson Hill next week is still going spare, if you want it."

Yep, I'd still never given Polly an answer to that. I mean, going to the gig; was that a perfect opportunity, or the worst idea ever?

"Roses and cherries," Mum whispers.

"Sugar sprinkles on top," I whisper back.

As Mum snuggles me to her chest, as everyone in Marigold Parade thinks they know how much Mum and I adore and trust each other, I'm quietly working out when exactly I can sneak off and key in the word *yes* to Polly Clarke's offer. . .

Saturday 19th May

Olive remembers her own two grannies vividly.

Both of them seemed to think being strict and severe was the ideal way to treat their grandkids, with plenty of smacks-on-the-bottom thrown in.

So it's no big surprise that Olive doesn't have happy memories of either of them, hates the title "gran" or "granny" and prefers me just to call her by her first name.

I'd never tell her but I do sometimes think she has inherited a *touch* of their strictness. I mean, I love Olive, but I don't think it's going to be easy having her living here with me while Mum's at the Manor House.

"Don't know why Queenie likes to collect these things," Olive grumbles, standing with her hands on her wide hips and glowering at the collection of 1950s clay poodle ornaments on the mantelpiece. "The flat's *way* too cluttered. Makes it seem *smaller* than it is."

"You *know* Mum and me like lots of colour and clutter," I tell her, pulling her wheeled suitcase through to Mum's room.

All Mum's amazing, kooky taste would go great in Alexa's house, I realize now that I've hung out there for the last four Saturday nights. My room would be the one at the top, the one Alexa's twin brother has at the moment. Not that I've seen Marley since that first time; he obviously has better, *cooler* things to do than hang around when I'm there.

"Still, I might rearrange a few things while she's away, just to cut down on dusting," says Olive, determined to get her own way.

Aargh! It's my home too, if she hadn't *noticed*.

BUZZ-BUZZ . . . BUZZZZZZZZZZZ.

"I'll get it," I call out, as I prop Olive's suitcase in Mum's bedroom.

I press the intercom, recognizing Freddie's coded two-shorts-and-a-long ring.

"Thank you for saving me from Olive!" I hiss at him as he bounds up the stairs.

I grab his T-shirt, slam the flat door shut and drag him into my room before he has time to say hello.

"It's Freddie! He's just come to help me out with some homework," I call out to my gran.

"Aw, do I have to?" he says, wrinkling his nose and flopping on to his back on the bed. "I'm *tired*. Mum and Dad have had me serving all day. I'm bored of working and smelling of fried egg. . ."

I lean over and sniff him – he's been in the shower. He smells deliciously fresh, of apple shampoo and toothpaste.

"You're fine," I tell him, "and anyway I don't have any homework to do. I just said that – *eeek*!"

Freddie's taken advantage of me being off-balance and yanked me down on to the bed. He's rolled over and is kneeling above me, pinning my arms above my head with one hand and tickling me *madly* with the other.

"Gerroff! *Nooooo!* Stop, Freddie, STOP!!" I giggle.

Before he'd arrived, I'd been looking through my box under the bed at the stupid – and stupidly *small* – collection of Dad Stuff. The postcard, the photo, the ring, the guitar pick. They're all I have of him. Mum threw everything else of his out – including photos – the day we moved here. I understand that she was angry and hurt, but I wish she hadn't. There's a chance I might be seeing Dad this time next week, even if it's just from a distance, and I'd've loved to have more of an idea what he looked like, once upon a time.

In fact, I'd been about to show the stuff to Freddie just now, before he broke into an unfair bout of tickle wrestling. . .

"Freddie – EEEK! I said GET *OFF*!"

"Doesn't sound like any homework's getting done in *here*," Olive's voice comes from the doorway. She's trying to look stern but I can see she's sort of smiling. She *adores* Freddie, though he drives her crazy by wearing jeans with holes in the knees and refusing her offers to stitch them up.

"I was just *testing* something, Olive," he says, pushing himself up to standing and flicking his floppy, slightly damp, apple-scented hair off his face.

"Testing what?" asks Olive, as I sit up and get my breath back – and surreptitiously kick the shoebox of Dad Stuff under the bed before Olive sees it and disapproves.

"Testing to see if Flo's just as tickly as usual," Freddie grins.

"*Very* funny, I don't think," growls Olive, but she's smiling in spite of herself. "How about you two do something more useful? Like go downstairs to the Chowdris' and get some snacks for tonight?"

"Tonight?" I say, my heart sinking as I see the five-pound note in her hand. "It's just that I'm going around to Alexa's. . ."

"But *Queenie* will be on," Olive huffs. "It's one thing to have watched all those audition shows with your new friends, Flo, but you should watch your mother here with your family!"

She's pointing at Freddie, including him in that sentence. But lovely as he is, he's not my family, any more than Polly and Heidi are. And *he* doesn't mind if we don't all squeeze on our lumpy old sofa to watch TV together just this once (OK, so it's been *more* than once that I haven't been around to join in).

But like I've said before, Freddie never minds about *anything*.

"Hey, I've got an idea," he blurts out now. "Why don't you move in with that Alexa girl, Flo?"

"Huh?" I laugh, not really sure where his joke is going.

"Well, then you could hang out with your posh friends in that flashy house *all* the time," he carries on. "Hey, maybe you'd let me and Zee come visit you. We'd use the servants' entrance, of course!"

Ha – he's just goofing, as usual.

But Olive is too busy scowling at me to listen to his jokes. Still, it's not as if this is a crucial *Big Dreams* tonight – they're only going to show the montages of Nathan Reed visiting all the contestants, telling them the good or bad news about the Manor House stage.

And as we were all actually *there* in Armando's when Nathan broke the news to Mum, I don't see why Olive's so bothered.

Luckily, I'm saved from Olive's continued scowling (and Freddie's strangely sarky humour) by the bell once again – three straight buzzes in a row.

Sounds like Zee's version of the code-ring, I think as I bound towards the intercom, press the release button and hear the street door thunk open below.

I yank the flat door ajar and yell, "Come on up!"

Please, please hurry and help me out here, I think, knowing that down-to-earth Zee will help defuse the sudden double-trouble atmosphere.

"Hi! Flo? Flo Brown? I'm Annie West. I just wanted to ask you a few questions, if that's all right?"

"What?" I jibber, staring at this stranger, this woman in a navy suit, and the guy behind her on the stairs holding a camera.

"We have it on good authority that your mum, Queenie, is one of the finalists going through to the next round of the *Big Dreams* competition. How does that make you feel?"

Flash! goes the camera.

"Huh? What 'good authority'?" I ask, totally thrown and not even understanding what that means. "Mum getting through; it's a secret – no one's meant to know till the show this evening."

"A close personal friend gave us the heads up, Flo," beams the reporter, using a term I don't properly understand either. "So, you're delighted, right?"

"What's going on?" says Freddie, appearing by my side in the doorway.

"Oh, is this your boyfriend?" smiles the woman.

"No!" we both say together.

"You two, in, *now*," barks Olive. She may be smaller – and rounder – than us, but she's pretty fearsome when she wants to be.

Suddenly shaking, I run into my room, with Freddie following.

"But Mrs Brown . . . it *is* Mrs Brown, isn't it?" I hear the woman's voice continue. "With your daughter Queenie's success so far on *Big Dreams*, we're keen to get our facts straight about her family and—"

"*Out!*" Olive orders them. "Please leave *now*."

"C'mere," says Freddie, his sarcasm from a minute ago now swapped for concern. I give in to his comforting hug. "But who are they?"

"Reporters," I mumble. "He *said* they'd come sniffing around."

"Yeah? *Who* said they'd come sniffing around?" asks Freddie, rocking me gently on the spot.

"Marley," I sniff, realizing I'm crying with the shock of being – what's it called? – doorstepped.

The rocking stops.

The arms drop away.

"He's the one who hangs out with Polly and Heidi, yeah?"

"Well, yes," I say, wondering why a weird atmosphere's sprung up all of a sudden.

"Why are you so into that lot, Flo?" Freddie suddenly bursts out. "Can't you see they've only been interested in you since they got a whiff of the fact that your mum might end up *famous*?"

What? Where's my funny, goofball Freddie gone?

"Whatever," he mutters darkly. "Mum and Dad could probably still do with a hand."

With that he leaves, excusing his way past Olive and the persistent journalist on the doorstep.

Hey, do I get the feeling that there *are* things that carefree Freddie cares about?

Like me having *other* friends besides him and Zee. . . ?

JUNE

Saturday 2nd June

My legs are like jelly and I'm shaking as I walk alongside the long queue stretching down the high street.

The newly restored red, green and cream art deco tiles of the Astoria Theatre are gleaming, but my eyes are too busy scanning for Polly and everyone to take it in properly.

When I texted her to let her know I was running late, she said they'd join the queue and I could meet them there. But what am I going to do about this shaking? I've *got* to make it stop before Polly and Heidi and the others take one look at me and think I'm having a meltdown.

Though I think maybe I *am* having a meltdown. . .

The mobile in my dungaree dress pocket jangles, rattling me even further. I yank it out, but my trembling fingers nearly drop it.

But there . . . there's a number that instantly makes me happier-than-happy and yet *more* stressed than ever.

"Mum?" I say.

She's calling me from the Manor House. It's an outgoing number only – all the acts living in the house are NOT to be disturbed, and are NOT allowed to have their own mobile phones with them, in case news from the Outside World seeps in and affects their confidence. All us relatives and friends have been told (make that *warned*) by the *Big Dreams* production team to keep our chats with contestants light and happy.

In other words, Mum – along with the others who got through to this stage – is living in a bubble. A bubble that mustn't be burst by weird, worrisome or bad news.

"Hey, my baby girl!"

All of a sudden, hearing Mum's voice makes me feel about five years old. I *really* want a hug.

"Hi," I squeak, hoping she can't hear the tears catch in my throat.

"Are you all right, Flo?"

She noticed.

"Just missing you a bit," I say, which isn't a lie, but

isn't the truth by a *long* way. "How's it going?"

Mum's called us a couple of times since she went into the Manor House. She's told us how hard the coaches are making them work ("It's a *lot* tougher than doing a few wash-and-blow-dries at Armando's"), and how nice the other contestants are ("But there're so many of us; I still don't know everyone"). The rooms are OK ("They're more like dorms; it's like being at Mallory Towers") and the food is amazing ("Beats the Beanz Café any day!").

In return, me and Olive have told her that everything's fine (sort of, when journalists aren't on the doorstep), we're getting on great as flatmates (debatable), that everyone in Marigold Parade is rooting for her and can't wait to watch her on TV this evening, when it's the second of the Manor House shows, but the first one featuring a lot of Mum (well, maybe not *everyone* on Marigold Parade will be watching tonight, i.e., *me*).

"It's all good, I guess. Tiring, though. *Really* tiring. And I don't know if I'll ever get used to cameras following me around."

"So who gets dropped from the competition tonight?" I ask, hoping my nosiness will make me sound normal. I know she knows, 'cause the filming's been done all through the week.

"Sorry, Flo – the *Big Dreams* team would *kill* me if I told you that!" Mum laughs. "You'll just have to watch and see, won't you?"

Well, one thing's for sure, it can't be *Mum* who's been voted off by the judges, and had to hand back her Golden Ticket. Otherwise she'd be at home, unpacking her bags.

"But hey – enough of me and what *I'm* doing. Tell me what's been going on with *you*, Flo."

Several things are going on with me, and all of them have left me shaking.

In order, they go like this:

1) Freddie isn't talking to me.
2) Zee isn't talking to me.
3) Olive isn't talking to me.
4) During the course of this evening, I *might* see my dad (gulp).

"I'm just on my way to meet Polly and everyone," I say, leaving her to assume I'm going to Alexa's house, and not the Astoria Theatre, to stare from a distance at my long-missing father.

Obviously, the *Big Dreams* production team

wouldn't class *that* as "light" or "happy" news.

I hadn't been planning on telling Olive about the Astoria gig either. Only Freddie and Zee knew, because we tell one another everything, don't we?

But then my secret slipped out in Zee's shop earlier today, right at Olive's feet, you could say.

I was buying a packet of biscuits for Armando's Ladies when Freddie barged in for some emergency supplies for the café.

"So? How are you feeling about tonight, Flo?" he'd asked me more loudly than he needed to.

He either didn't see or just ignored the panicked widening of my eyes as I tried to silently warn him to shut up.

(Y'know, I think it might have been a case of *ignoring*; he's been a bit funny with me all week. Since I told him I was going to the concert with Polly and her mates, in fact.)

"Have you planned what you're going to say if you run into your dad?" he blithely and *loudly* carried on.

It was at that point that Olive stepped out from behind the shelving unit with a bottle of bleach in her hand and a dark glower on her face.

I yelled at Freddie for blowing my cover.

He stormed out.

Zee told me off (!) for blaming him.

I snapped at her.

She stormed into the back of the shop.

Olive told me to get back to work, and that we'd be having "words" at teatime.

I'm still shaking from Olive's "words". I've never been called "stupid" and "thoughtless" and "irresponsible" by her before.

And I'm shaking at the fact that I told her it didn't matter what she thought, I was *still* going to the concert and she couldn't stop me.

Then I'd rushed out of the flat, frantically texting Polly to let her know I was on my way.

Oh, where are they? I think, scanning the crowded queue for Polly, Heidi, Alexa or Gabrielle's familiar faces as I keep Mum clamped to my ear. I'd even be grateful to see Marley's moody face, if it meant I'd found my friends.

"I don't know *how* I'll come across on TV tonight," her comforting voice says now. "They were even filming us when we were brushing our teeth. Can you believe it? Ah . . . I'm getting told my vocal coach is ready for me. Saturday night and I've *still* got to work. Slave drivers – ha! Anyway, I'll have to go. . . But everything *is* all right, isn't it, Flo?"

That last question *actually* means: "You haven't heard anything from your dad, have you? You would tell me, wouldn't you, Flo?"

But we're not going to get into that. I have to protect her; stop her from even *thinking* about Dad while she's concentrating on her big break.

"Everything's fine, really," I try to reassure her, even though I'm scared my teeth might start chattering in a minute, I'm shaking so much.

"Oh, good," she says, sounding relieved. "Well, I'll try to check in for a proper chat in the morning, yeah?"

"Sure," I tell her, thinking that I'll have to get up really early and watch the show that I set to record before I left. (Olive was in the kitchen, banging pots and plates around in the sink, taking her frustration out on defenceless dirty dishes instead of me.)

"Bye, honey – love you."

"Love you – bye. . ." I mutter to Mum, my voice cracking.

I press the end-call button and stop dead on the pavement. The only things moving are the tears streaming down my face.

"Flo?"

Someone has stepped out of the queue and is gripping me by the arms.

"C'mere, you," says a deep, friendly voice, and I'm in a big bear hug, koi carp swimming protectively around me. "What's up, Flo-Flo?"

"I'm the WORST daughter and the WORST granddaughter and the WORST friend," I sob into a black T-shirt with a giant skull on it.

"Hey, what are you talking about?" says Wolfie, his stubbly chin prickling the top of my head. "You're a great kid. Everyone knows that. You're having a bad day, that's all. It's probably 'cause your mum's away and—"

"It's not that!" I snuffle. "It's 'cause I'm here tonight. . ."

"Actually, what *are* you doing here?" Wolfie asks, slackening his hug enough to look down into my face. "And who are you with?"

"I'm supposed to be meeting some friends from school. They had a spare ticket," I hiccup. "But I came, because – because I wanted—"

"You wanted to see your dad. Right?" Wolfie fills in.

I stare up at him with overflowing eyes. "Mum doesn't know I'm here."

"But she knows you've been thinking about him; she's told me." Wolfie's been Mum's best friend since he opened the Tattoo Den five years ago. They admired each other's tattoos. She showed him the one she hated – the tiny pony on her wrist – and he offered to cover it over with the black lily. When somebody helps you like that, helps you get over a constant reminder of bad stuff, you know you can trust that person, I guess.

"OK, you're coming with me," says Wolfie, dropping his arms but taking my hand. "Hey, David – I'll see you inside, OK?"

As I'm hurried away, I see the bloke Wolfie is talking to – someone wearing jeans and a mod-style button-down top – and realize he looks vaguely familiar.

"I wasn't planning on being here tonight, but I was chatting to David today and he said he had a spare ticket," Wolfie explains, though I wasn't asking. My muddled head is too busy wondering what's happening.

And then it dawns on me that "David" is D.B. Gregory, the accountant whose office is next door to the Tattoo Den. I've only ever seen him in suits and ties, though I can't say I've ever really noticed him properly before.

"What – what are we doing?" I ask, as Wolfie squeezes me through the queue with a flurry of "excuse me, mate"s and bundles me down an alley at the side of the theatre.

I'm nervous and confused, though it's also a relief to have someone else taking charge for once.

"We're not dragging this on – *that's* what we're doing," he answers firmly, explaining nothing, as far as I'm concerned.

Up ahead is a big metal fire door, propped open with a wheeled metal case. The case has the Crimson Hill logo stencilled on it, and a wiry guy with a baseball cap and low-slung trousers is about to push it inside.

What's Wolfie planning on doing? I fret.

"Hey!" he calls out to the wiry bloke with the bum crack on display. "Is Horse around?"

I never say his name; I always call him Dad. To say or think his name makes him uncomfortably real. So real, he could be just around the corner. Which, of course, he very probably is.

Help. . .

"Horse?" says the guy. "Nah, mate. There's been some problem –he's not here for this show."

Oh, I see.

OK.

Since I saw that piece in the *Herald* at the beginning of the year, I've been wound up in tangles of jangling, conflicting feelings. And those rigid-as-barbed-wire tangles have tightened to breaking point today.

Till now; now that I've heard he's not even *here*.

The tension tangles suddenly melt like they're made of warm caramel.

And I'm melting with them, blackness and the pavement rushing up to meet me. . .

Horse.

How stupid a name is that for a dad?

Though his real name is Harvey Cook.

He got the "Horse" nickname at school.

"Your mum told me that he never knew why they called him that, but that's boys for you," Wolfie chats away. "I mean, look at me! *I* can't remember why my best mates started calling me Wolfie. And I can't remember why I nicknamed them Froggie and Mental. . ."

Both of us should be watching Crimson Hill right now. But somewhere in the rows of cheering fans packed into the Astoria, there's an empty seat beside the guy from the accountant's office and another beside Polly, Heidi, Gabrielle, Alexa and Marley.

I didn't care about missing the band, though. I know everyone's meant to love them because they're such legends and everything, but I've never really liked Crimson Hill's music – the lead singer's way too shouty for me.

All I'd wanted to do was stare at the stage before Crimson Hill even came on. I'd planned to scan the faces of the crew that were setting up, sound-checking the instruments, making sure the mics were live.

I'd wanted to watch the faces of guys "*One-two, one-two*"-ing into the mics, in case one of those faces was my dad's.

My dad, Horse.

The roadie.

He'd given up his own attempts at being a musician (and a father, I guess) and taken the chance to be part of the behind-the-scenes crew for Crimson Hill, touring the world with them. Actually, touring the world with them about *five times* now (I Wikipedia'd the band a while back).

But how useless was it that he wasn't there the one time they play in MY hometown?!

"Why do you think he wasn't working tonight,

of all nights?" I ask Wolfie now. I'm leaning against him. He's the only thing that's solid and comfy right now. A bit like a dad should be, I guess – but I've never had much experience in that area, have I?

"That I do not know, Flo, babe," says Wolfie. His muscly arm is around me and he gives me a squeeze. The guy with the baseball cap at the backstage door didn't tell us any more – he was too busy running inside to find a St John's Ambulance person to attend to me.

And now we're here at the A&E department of the hospital, waiting to make sure that I didn't get concussion when I fainted.

"Flo? Flo Brown?" says a doctor in a white coat, appearing by our side.

"Yes," I mumble, suddenly feeling shy and stupidly young. *And* stupid.

"So what have you been up to, then?" he asks, clicking his pen as if he's about to make notes.

Ha.

Where do I start? And how's it going to sound if I tell the doctor that I was on a wild goose chase for a horse?

"She fainted at a gig," Wolfie jumps in and explains more simply.

"Ah, Crimson Hill!" the doctor nods. "We've got another couple of people in here from that already. Probably have a few more by the end of the evening. Overheating, dehydration . . . it's always the same with big events and crowds. Want to come with me and we'll take a look at you, Flo?"

Wolfie puts his arm protectively around me in case I get a case of the wobbles and we follow the doctor to a bed, surrounded by curtains with a pattern so jolly it could give you a *serious* headache.

With a couple of whooshes, the doctor pulls the curtains shut, creating a private space. Though I can just make out someone in the curtained cubicle next to mine, where the material didn't quite meet up.

Whoever's in there must be in a worse state than me; they're lying down. At least the doctor has just asked me to sit on the edge of *my* bed, which makes me feel less ill.

"Are you her father?" the doctor asks as he shines a blinding torch into my left eye.

"No, I'm just a frien—"

"I'm her grandmother!" Olive barks, bustling through a gap in the curtains and coming straight for me like a small, round, squidgy missile, her plum-coloured bob swinging agitatedly. "Are you all right, Flo, darling? Is she all right, doctor?"

In the muddle of the moment and Olive's relieved cuddles I feel tearful again, glad that I'm once more her darling, after today's "words".

"I think she'll be fine," the doctor assures Olive. "But we just need to run a few checks, to be on the safe side."

And with that, Olive now bustles over to hug Wolfie, and I have a bright, blinding light shining in my eye once again, only the other one this time.

"Thanks for looking out for her, Wolfie," I hear Olive say, as I try desperately not to blink at the dazzling whiteness pinging off the back of my retina.

"Looks all right in there," the doctor mutters. "Now I'll just come round the other side of the bed and feel that head of yours."

There can't be *too* much wrong with my skull; as the doctor's hands move around, it feels a little like having a head massage.

At the same time, I stare at the gap in the curtains, trying to blink away the brightness and swirls the torch beam left behind.

"Right, let's get you to X-ray," I hear a nurse's voice say in the curtained cubicle next to mine, and I see the bed moving, being wheeled away. "We'll soon have you sorted, Mr. . ."

Her voice overlaps with the squeak of wheels on the lino floor.

But just for a second there, my psychedelic gaze rests on the pained expression of the man on the trolley. His face, turned sideways towards me, is contorted in pain. His eyes glance my way without seeing me, and an extended "*Owwwwww. . .!*" comes out of his mouth.

It makes me feel like a fake; I'm just some silly girl who got herself so worked up she fainted.

The doctor more or less decides the same thing, and half an hour and a bunch more checks later, he lets us leave with instructions for ice, painkillers, rest – and to come straight back if there're any problems.

"Well, there's no real damage done, so let's not bother your mother with this, eh, Flo?" says Olive, patting my hand as we sit together in the back of the taxi that Wolfie has put us in, before he headed off to join David the accountant and catch the end of Crimson Hill's show.

Thinking of Wolfie's various kindnesses, I mutter, "That was nice of Wolfie to call you to come to the hospital."

"Oh, he didn't call me," says Olive. "I saw you getting into the ambulance, and Mr Gregory the accountant gave me a lift in his car."

"What? But – but why were you there?" I ask, my not-quite-concussed head swimming.

"Well, you're only thirteen, Flo! I was hardly going to let you go into town to the concert on your own, so—"

"So you *followed* me?"

"If you like," Olive says sniffily. "I came along *behind* you, if you want to call that *following*. I planned to sit in the café across the road from the Astoria with my Sudoku, till the concert finished, and then I was going to collect you."

Before I went hunting for my dad, is what she means.

"But then I saw you go off with Wolfie and I had to run over and ask that Mr Gregory – David – what was going on. He wasn't sure, so we looked around for a few minutes, and then we see you and Wolfie being taken away in an ambulance. Next thing, David is taking me to the multi-storey car park and – whoosh – he speeds me to the hospital, bless him."

Bless him, bless Wolfie, bless Olive and her undercover operation to keep me safe. (What's the symbol for the SAS? Maybe Wolfie could tattoo it on her arm. . .)

I sit quietly, trying to take it all in. But it's only as the cab slows down into Marigold Parade that I start to worry that I might have hit my head harder than anyone's realized.

'Cause I've suddenly imagined something that can't be true.

Back in the A&E ward, when the man on the trolley was being wheeled away. . .

"We'll soon have you sorted," I'd heard the nurse say.

"Mr Cook," she'd added.

I can't *really* have heard her say that name above the loud squeak of the trolley wheels, can I?

Can I?

I don't care what the doctor says.

To imagine I heard my dad's name; I *must* have concussion. . .

Sunday 3rd June

I am SO proud of my mum.

She is working SO hard at trying to improve her life, and mine too.

I SO understand that she has to concentrate one hundred per cent during these few weeks, and that I have to do my best not to miss her too madly.

I SO get why Olive says we should keep the whole Crimson Hill/hospital drama quiet, and not stress Mum out with it.

But lying here with my face in my pillow, I SO, SO, *SO* want to hug her and have her hug me right back. . .

"Fancy a bit of company, Flo?" I hear Olive's voice ask now.

She must be standing in my bedroom doorway, but I don't lift my head to look. I'm sort of hoping I might quietly smother myself to death. That way I won't have to feel so madly muddled with guilt (over keeping stuff from Mum), misery (my best friends don't like me any more), relief (that I didn't actually see my dad) and regret (er, 'cause I didn't actually see my dad).

"Sure about that?" says Olive, even though I haven't responded.

Weird. Olive's sounding unusually gentle and kind there.

"No, thanks," I say, turning my head enough to glance her way.

But it's not *Olive* who's standing in the doorway . . . it's Freddie and Zee.

They're grinning at me, and Freddie's holding on to a tray laden with stuff.

"Go on in, you two," Olive orders, standing behind them in the hall. "And for goodness' sake, get out of your bed when you've got visitors, Flo Brown!"

Now *that's* more like my gran.

I scramble to a sitting position and shove my messy Sunday-morning hair off my head. I can feel the heat of my cheeks as I remember me, Freddie and Zee sniping at one another yesterday in Zee's parents' shop.

"Right, I'll leave you three to make up," Olive says brusquely, pulling my bedroom door closed.

"Your gran came into the shop this morning and told me what happened to you last night," says Zee, settling herself on the end of my bed. "And I told *him*, of course."

"Peace offering," Freddie grins now and sets the tray he's holding on to my bedside table. He's brought it up from the café – I recognize the mug for the tea and ribbed glass for the juice. And the blueberry muffin is sitting on a Beanz Café serviette.

"Mum sent these for you," says Zee, taking the glass plate of Indian treats off the tray and offering it to me.

"Ladoos," I murmur. I've tried lots of Mrs Chowdri's home-made sweets over the years, and these are my absolute favourite.

"Nope!" Zee growls, slapping away my reaching hand.

"What?" I say, a little shaken.

"You don't get one till you say we're all friends again!"

Well, that's a no-brainer. I never wanted to *stop* being friends. It was Zee and Freddie who seemed to be cross with *me*.

Then all of a sudden, out of the corner of my eye, just by my pillow, I see my on-mute phone vibrate with an incoming message. *Polly* is the name that glows out – she must be replying to the sorry-I-couldn't-make-it-to-the-gig message I sent her.

But in the current climate – i.e., making up with Freddie and Zee – I don't think it's the time to respond.

With a casual nudge of my pillow, it's covered.

"Ignore Ms Strict here, Flo," Freddie is saying to me, scooping up a little pastry and sticking it in my mouth before I can protest. "*I* started it. I shouldn't have blurted out that you were going to the concert, not when I knew your gran was in the shop."

So it *was* deliberate, then.

"Why?" is all I manage to mumble with my mouth full.

"Isn't it obvious, darling?" he says dramatically, throwing himself on the ground by my bedside and grabbing my hands in his. "I'm *madly* in love with you, Flo Brown, and I can't *bear* the idea of you spending time with Polly Clarke and all her fancy-pants posh buddies, especially if one of them's a *boy*!"

With that, he breaks into a high-pitched version of Lady Gaga's "Bad Romance" that's so loud it could wake the neighbours. (Except he *is* my neighbour.)

I'm caught between laughing and groaning and trying not to choke on my ladoo. I still don't completely understand why everything got so out of hand between us all in the Chowdri's shop yesterday, but I don't really care; I'm just happy we're all fooling around and being *us* again.

Glancing over at Zee, I expect to see her rolling her big doe eyes as Freddie sing, sing, sings his way through the entire song. But instead, she's staring at me.

"The lyrics to this are interesting, aren't they?"

"Um, I suppose," I answer her with a shrug, thinking they're a bit random and crazy, like most of Lady Gaga's songs.

But Zee seems to have lost interest and is doing something far more important, i.e., grabbing one of the cushions piled on my bed and giving Freddie a friendly thwack around the head with it. . .

Saturday 16th June

"*Sugar! Dah-dah-DAH-dah-DAH-dah*. . ."

Freddie thunks down beside me at the table, singing a snatch of an old track from the sixties by some band called the Archies.

The song fits: first, because he's just brought me a bowl piled high with gleaming white sugar lumps for my tea. Second, it's the track Mum's been working on with her vocal coaches. She'll be performing it live next Saturday night as part of the Solo Singers show at some fancy theatre in the centre of London.

There'll be four of us in the audience watching: me, Olive, Armando and Wolfie. Olive is hysterically excited, but hiding it well with a mask of extra grumpiness. In between fixing zips and hems at the dry-cleaner's, she's sewing a banner with patchwork letters that spell out "QUEENIE", while growling at Bernard or Philip or anyone who comes near and distracts her.

I can't wait either. Watching Mum on TV is mind-blowing enough. Seeing her sing right in front of me, with lights and dancers . . . it gives me goosebumps on my goosebumps just imagining it.

"Freddie – you're putting off the customers with that yodelling of yours," his mum Angie shouts from behind the counter.

"Mum, apart from Flo there *are* no customers," Freddie tells her.

"Exactly! They're probably all on their way in, then they hear *you* bellowing and turn right around."

Angie's smiling; she doesn't mean it. The Saturday morning breakfast "rush" is over (Wolfie and a few of the Ladies coming in for a fry-up) and it's usually pretty quiet till a few more of the women from the retirement houses wander in for a companionable lunch together.

I've just popped in for a hello before I start my shift at Armando's. I love that me and Freddie and Zee are as close as we've ever been after that weird blip of spiky words on the day of the Crimson Hill concert.

And to prove how important they are to me, last Saturday – despite the usual invite from Alexa – I watched the final Manor House show at home in Marigold Parade with Olive and Freddie, plus Zee remotely (she kept texting comments from her flat). The same's happening tonight for the Meet the Mentors show.

Polly and Heidi have seemed disappointed that I've not been around the last couple of weekends and keep asking if I'm all right, which is sweet of them. It's 'cause of the fainting thing on the night of the concert; they're assuming that I'm not a hundred per cent well, I think, rather than a hundred per cent emotionally wrung out after the last few months.

"Ah, here comes a section of your mum's fan club now," says Freddie, jumping up and opening the door for Mrs Jennings, Maureen and Mrs Georgiou.

"Ooh, Freddie, don't look at us till we're beautified!" Maureen jokes, patting her fading white curls.

She and the other Ladies are obviously having a cup of tea before they head through to Armando's, where I'll soon be serving them yet *more* tea.

"And how are you, Flo, love? Doing all right without your mum?" asks Mrs Jennings with a concerned tilt of her head.

She's talking about the fact that Mum's taken the advice of the *Big Dreams* team and is staying on in a hotel in London. Well, when I say *advice*, they told her she absolutely *had* to, if she was serious about keeping her place in the competition.

"Yes, I'm fine, thanks," I say brightly, then quickly rifle in my bag for the mobile I can hear jingling with a text message.

I've become such an expert at secrets and lies this year. Right now I'm both lying and hiding the guilty secret that I can't help resent Mum for choosing *Big Dreams* over *me*.

As for Dad, well, I don't know why he wasn't around for the Astoria gig, but I noseyed on the band's website and saw that they're in Holland now, as part of their European tour, before they head off to Australia.

Horse will be getting further and further away from me – even if he never got near in the first place. . .

"Just think – you'll see her at the live show next week," Mrs Georgiou adds. "You must be *so* excited, Flo."

"Yes, it'll be amazing," I say, though I don't know how I feel about the fact that we're not allowed to meet up in person. Olive's had a chat with one of the production team, who explained that *pre*-show, the contestants need to concentrate, and then *post*-show, they'll be whisked off to be interviewed for the spin-off results programme that's on telly straight after.

Plinky-plinky-plink-plink!

Finally, I locate the phone in the corner of my bag, and see a text . . . from a number I don't recognize.

"Who is it?" Freddie asks, casually interested and probably expecting it to be from Zee all of next-door-away.

"Dunno," I mumble, flipping to the message.

Hi, it's Marley. Got your number from my sister, Alexa. Have you seen the Sun *today? If not, get it. . .*

"What?" says Freddie, who must have seen my face go white with panic. "Who is it?"

"It's Polly," I lie. "He, I mean *she*, says there's

136

something I need to see in the newspaper. The *Sun*. . ."

Freddie leaps into action. "Mum – do we have a copy of the *Sun*?"

"No – we've just got the *Mirror* and the *Mail* and—"

Angie hasn't even finished and Freddie has hurtled out of the door.

"What's wrong, dear?" asks Mrs Jennings.

"I'm not sure," I say, beginning to shake a little. "There was a reporter nosing around awhile back, but Olive told her to go away. Nothing happened after that, so I thought it was OK."

But hadn't Marley warned me not so long ago that the press would come sniffing and snooping if Mum began to do well? And here he was, letting me know it had actually happened. *Personally* letting me know, rather than passing the message on via his sister or Polly or whoever. Why had he done that?

And why had I lied to Freddie about who the text was from? It's not as if I'd *liked* Marley the few times I'd met him. And I know Freddie was spoofing around with that "Bad Romance" routine last week when he and Zee and I were all making up, but it's not as if he likes me in the sort of way that would make him truly jealous of another boy. . .

"I got it!" Freddie yells, steaming back into the café. Behind him is Zee, bouncing her little brother Roo on her hip as she runs.

Freddie slaps the paper on the table and begins to flip through it, as Mrs Jennings, Mrs Georgiou and Maureen huddle round. Freddie's parents, Angie and Mario, hurry over too.

"*There,*" says Zee, pointing a slim finger at page five.

"*Big Dreams Favourite Queenie Deserted By Father of Her Child,*" the headline screams.

And beside it is a big photo of Mum, leaning thoughtfully on a piano during a rehearsal. Next to it is a photo of a bloke playing guitar on stage – Dad! My heart's still thudding at the sight of him when I notice the other, smaller photo on the page. It's a photo of *me*.

Those gates behind me; they're the *school* gates.

This is recent.

It's me and Zee, our arms linked – though Zee's mostly been cropped out.

Wow.

I had no idea someone was watching me, *stalking* me, taking my photo!

And look: below the photos, there it all is, sentence after raw sentence about me and Mum and our lives. Some of what is said is sort of true, but written in the most awful, exaggerated way.

"*Years on, Queenie still sometimes cries herself to sleep – 'it's hard to get over such a brutal betrayal,' says a close friend.*"

Huh? *What* close friend?

"How do the people at the newspaper know all this?" asks Freddie's dad.

"Because *someone's* gone and told them," says Zee.

I suddenly feel stalked and watched all over again. . .

Saturday 23rd June

"Oh my goodness," says Armando. "I don't know if my heart can stand the excitement!"

"Silly old fool," Olive grumbles next to me.

I give her a jab with my elbow. I know she wishes it was just her, me and Wolfie here in the audience at tonight's show, but each contestant was allocated four tickets, and Mum chose who she wanted here to support her.

And apart from respecting Mum's choices, Olive should also be grateful that Armando ended up part of our group; after all, he drove us to London, so we didn't have to get on a coach in our fancy clothes.

Speaking of fancy clothes, our versions of "fancy" vary quite a lot.

Armando is in a grey suit, white shirt and red bow tie. (He looks like he should be conducting the backing band.)

Olive is wearing a burnt orange trouser suit that was left uncollected at the dry-cleaner's for the last five years. ("Hope the owner doesn't come back for it now, since I've taken it in four sizes," she muttered earlier.)

Wolfie is wearing what he calls his "wedding outfit", 'cause he bought it when a friend of his got married. It's his usual T-shirt, jeans and biker boots, with the addition of an ankle-skimming black leather coat. (If his friend wasn't a goth, that might be a weird wedding outfit choice, I guess.)

As for me, I'm in my Olive-altered dungaree dress, but wearing it with black lacy tights and a pair of Mum's black pumps. (I knew she wouldn't mind if I borrowed them. Not that she's been around to ask.)

"Hey, ladies and gentlemen, boys and girls!" says a man on stage who's part of the production team, I think. "We'll be coming out of the pre-recorded video section in just a few seconds—"

We've been watching a montage of clips from the series so far, to the soundtrack of "Don't Stop Believing" by Journey. I smile to myself as I think of Freddie doing a version of it.

"—so let's have some quiet . . . followed by *very* loud cheering when Nathan comes back on to introduce tonight's final act."

There's a bit of excited hubbub, and then everyone goes suitably quiet as the music fades and the lights dim.

Everyone except Olive.

"Here – Wolfie," she barks. "Grab an end of this."

There're a few shushes (mostly from me) as Olive unfurls the patchwork "Queenie" banner in her lap. It has a pole at either end; *she's* holding one, and Wolfie does as he's told and holds the other. Me and Armando hunch a little lower in our seats, so we can see under it.

"Here we go, eh, Flo?" says Wolfie.

He's trying his best to make sure I'm having a good time. They all are in their own way, even if

Olive forgets herself for a minute and lapses back into grumbling and quibbling.

In the last couple of weeks, ever since that horrible piece in the *Sun*, Olive, Armando and Wolfie have rallied round. I'm not entirely sure who to trust at the moment (*someone* – as Zee pointed out – helped the journalist with their story) but I know for sure I can always depend on these three people.

Suddenly, there's another huge swell of music, followed by deafening applause, and Nathan Reed is bounding on to the stage wearing a shiny blue suit and a wide smile featuring breathtakingly white teeth.

"Hey, is this the best show on telly or what!" he booms to thunderous roars. "And we may have seen a few fantastic acts already this evening, but *boy* do we have a treat for you *now*."

More roaring.

Lots more roaring.

Olive and Wolfie and Armando, roaring.

I'm pretty sure I'm roaring too, but my voice is lost in the general noise.

"Because right now, I'd like to introduce to you the amazing, the super-talented, the ravishingly beautiful, the *delicious* MISS . . . QUEENIE . . . RAE . . . *BROWN*!!!"

The crowd go crazy with every word Nathan Reed says – *except* for me, Olive, Armando and Wolfie.

I can just tell we all felt the same there.

"Amazing" was good.

"Super-talented" was well-deserved.

"Ravishingly beautiful" sounded a little *meh*.

"Delicious" was plain *creepy*, the way he'd just said it.

I didn't like any strange bloke, especially one in a nasty shiny suit and overbleached teeth, talking about my mum like that, and you can bet that mother-hen Olive, protective Armando and quietly lovelorn Wolfie feel the same.

And then there was Maureen. Yesterday evening I'd gone knocking on the doors of the retirement homes, asking the Ladies to sign a good-luck card for Mum. "That Nathan what's-his-name; he's got a thing for our Queenie, hasn't he?" she said disapprovingly. "But he's one of them famous types that like the sound of their own voices. You tell him to keep away from our Queenie, OK?"

I'd wanted to hug her when she said that. I know most people would think I was completely *mad* not to be excited at having a celebrity flirting with your mother, but I haven't enjoyed watching the way he's been so touchy-feely with Mum in their Manor House chats.

And I haven't much liked the way Mum's talked about him in her occasional calls. He's been giving her heaps of advice, apparently.

Taking her aside for cups of coffee and friendly chats.

Hmm. . .

It's just that I have this sinking feeling Mum might have too many sparkles in her eyes and be impressed by the attention of the famous Nathan Reed.

And I have a feeling that he might be keen on my mum because she's gorgeous and talented – *and* currently the favourite to win the *Big Dreams* competition.

But there's no time to dwell on it; the spotlight fades on Nathan Reed as he steps aside, and a figure – a perfect silhouette with a towering beehive – steps forward from the darkness into the warmth of gold-coloured shafts of light and applause.

"'*Sugar!*'" Mum belts out suddenly, as the band launches into the tune simultaneously.

With that she zips into the Archies song, girls appearing around her in cropped leggings and stripy tops, doing sixties-style dance moves.

She's . . . electrifying. Her voice is powerful but not shouty. She smiles so much as she sings that her dimples go supersonic, surely hypnotizing everyone who's watching, if they haven't already melted at the sound coming out of her mouth.

Her make-up is perfect, a black pencilled beauty spot added to her already cartoon-cute look.

The soft red velvet rose in her hair exactly matches the inked roses tumbling down her left arm, and she's wearing cute red wedge shoes that I've never seen before.

"What HAS she got on?" Olive hisses loudly in my ear, slightly spoiling the moment.

I don't want to waste a second of my Mum-watching time (I haven't seen her – except for on a TV screen – in weeks now), but I know what Olive means.

Mum's not dressed in her own clothes tonight; a stylist must have told her what she should put on. And what she's put on is a vaguely vintage-looking red ball gown, but – being the daughter of a vintage fanatic and the granddaughter of a seamstress –

I can tell it's all wrong; the material is cheap and new, the colour brash. It doesn't quite fit her around the waist either. And anyway, Mum *never* wears dresses, and looks to me to be a tiny bit uncomfortable in it. Naturally, I've seen her dance (round the living room with me or Wolfie, or round Armando's with one or other of the Ladies), but she seems stiff up there on the stage, despite the great vocal performance she's giving.

But before I can process any of my fuzz of thoughts properly, the three minutes of the song are over and Mum is bowing deep, waves of cheering and clapping washing over her.

"Whoooooh-hoooo! How about *that*, ladies and gentlemen, boys and girls," whoops Nathan Reed, running on from the side of the stage JUST as Mum straightens up from her bow.

I grab the middle of the patchwork banner and wiggle it, desperate for her to see it, to see us, to see *me*.

"So, come on; how do you feel after that, Queenie?" Nathan asks my happy but slightly overwhelmed mother.

"Good, thanks!" she answers breathlessly, sweeping back a tendril of dark hair that's come loose. "Though I'd feel better if I knew where my daughter is right now!"

My heart practically *explodes* as I see Mum putting a hand to her forehead and scanning the audience.

For the first time in a very long time, I feel like a little kid – a little kid who really, *really* wants her mother. Now.

In a sudden rush, I'm on my feet waving, and am about to yell "I'm HERE, Mum!" when Nathan Reed booms in with "Well, I'm sure she's proud of you, you STAR!" and does what he's never done before, to any of the contestants in *any* of the previous three years' worth of shows.

With the audience breaking into sudden and surprised shrieks and yelps of approval, Nathan Reed lifts my mother up and spins, spins, *spins* her around.

I'm not sure who's growling the loudest (Wolfie or Olive) or who's frowning the hardest (Armando or me), but it feels like we four are most definitely in the minority in this vast audience.

An audience of people here – and probably all over the UK – who think they've maybe, perhaps, just *possibly* witnessed the budding of the latest celebrity romance.

Please, please, *no*. . .

JULY

Friday 13th July

"Isn't it lovely?"

"Won't it be brilliant?"

"A whole day, together, just you and me!"

"Can't wait till Friday – can you, my little Flo-Flo?"

Those are the phrases I clearly remember Mum saying when she floored me at the beginning of the week with one phone call.

We were going to meet up.

Me and her.

In London.

I know!

She and Olive had chatted already while I was at school and sorted the whole thing out. Olive would put me on the coach to London at 10 a.m., and Mum would pick me up at Victoria Bus Station. At 3 p.m., Mum would put me on the coach home, and Olive would meet me.

"That's four hours . . . not exactly a whole day," Zee had pointed out when I went screeching down to the shop to tell her, 'cause she likes to be exact and truthful, even when I don't want to hear it. (She'd still high-fived me, though.)

"Wow, checking out the 'designer' shops in the West End? Going to an 'exclusive' restaurant? Get *you*, Flo!" Freddie had teased me, doing the inverted commas in the air, when I'd hurtled into the café next to spread the good news.

"Great! But, er, doesn't that mean you're skiving or bunking off or whatever you call it?" said Wolfie when I told him, sounding surprisingly like a concerned parent. "'Cause I thought schools weren't into you doing that kind of thing. . ."

To be honest, I'd fretted about missing a day of school as well. But when I'd said so to Olive, she'd told me it was fine – Mum had assured her that she'd already arranged it and OK'd it with my head teacher.

So it was full-steam ahead to Friday!

My special, wonderful (chunk of a) day alone with Mum. . .

"Oh, bless them!" she says now.

We're in this sleek-looking restaurant at the

top of an art gallery, with amazing views over the River Thames. There are vast bouquets of lilies everywhere. The menu was confusing at first but the food turned out to be gorgeous (they've promised my "Soft Meringue With Blood Orange Sorbet" will be here any second).

Mum has just clapped her hands to her face as I tell her about the Ladies and their new habit of having a regular sing-song at Armando's, crooning along together to every old track that comes on the radio, since Mum's not around to entertain them. It's the sweetest thing: a bunch of warbly high voices, with Armando's booming baritone joining in.

What makes it even *more* fun is seeing the obvious pain on Roxanne and Valerie's faces whenever they launch into another tune.

"Well, they miss you," I tell her, not wanting to upset her – or myself – by saying that I miss her too. "I guess they just get lonely in their little houses, and that's why they all love coming to get their hair done and have some—"

"Oh I nearly forgot!" Mum suddenly interrupts my tales of home. "I have *another* surprise for you."

I'm not sure that I *want* another surprise. There've

been a couple already today and I haven't much liked them, to be honest.

First, there was no waving, loving mum waiting to meet me at Victoria Bus Station this morning – just a clipped and efficient girl called Chloe from the *Big Dreams* production team. "Queenie's been at a vocal workshop," she told me brusquely as she sped me through the teeming streets of London in her car. "I'm taking you straight to the store to meet up with her."

The "store" was some hyper-trendy shop with no price tags on anything.

"Why don't they just say how much their stuff is?" I'd whispered to Mum.

"Honey, it's just because everything's so high end, yeah?" said India, butting in on my whisper.

India is the *Big Dreams* stylist. She was swooping Mum around a few "high end" stores to see if there were things they'd lend her to wear for the semi-final show in just over a week's time. The semi-final show I wasn't going to be allowed to attend, it turned out.

"It's a new format. Celebrity audience only at the semi-final, yeah?" India said to me as we waited outside the changing room for Mum.

Well, no, I hadn't known that, actually (hello to

my *second* surprise). I'd assumed me and Olive and Armando and Wolfie might be there to cheer Mum on again. How silly of me. . .

"Ta-da!" Mum trills brightly, pointing at something behind me in the restaurant.

I turn and blink, as it's pretty light and bright in this place.

Or maybe it's just the white teeth.

"Flo! Good to meet you! Heard so much about you! How're you doing? Had a good day so far?"

Nathan Reed.

It seems I am having lunch – or at least pudding – with Nathan Reed.

Everyone at school would go spectacularly *nuts* right now if they knew this was happening.

I would go nuts, if I didn't think this guy was a bit . . . *icky*, famous or not.

"S'OK," I say, in a voice that I know is no bigger than a mouse squeak.

"Flo!" Mum laughs nervously, nudging me in the ribs 'cause she's thinking I can do so much better. "You don't know it, but you owe Nathan a *huge* thank you."

I do? I think to myself, tying the linen napkin in my lap into knots.

"*He* is the one who made today happen," Mum starts to explain. "*He* is the one who said to the production team, 'Queenie needs to—'"

"—spend time with her kid," Nathan finishes off for her, nodding his head and looking . . . well, *smug*.

"*Daughter*," Mum gently corrects him. "In fact, Nathan is the one who put in the call to your head teacher to get the go-ahead for you to miss a day of school."

My heart is twisting as much as the napkin in my hand.

"Thanks," I say in my mouse-squeak.

"I know you probably think we've all stolen your mother away from you, Flo, but you do realize she's going to be a star, yeah?"

Bright white teeth – that's all I can see when he talks.

"Um, y-y-yeah," I stutter, not feeling like me, so far from Marigold Parade, so far from Mum, even if she *is* sitting right across from me.

"Good for you! *Good for you!*" he says to me, in that way I recognize from TV, when he pats contestants on the hand who have just been voted off.

Then the hand that's been patting mine flies off as he goes to check his bleeping mobile.

"Excuse me, miss," a young and smiley waitress says to me. "Soft meringue and—"

"Sorry!" Nathan says, clicking his phone off and putting his hand between me and the waitress trying to deliver my dessert. "The kid's car's here."

"Already?" says Mum, clearly disappointed that our time is up.

She starts gathering up her jacket and bag to come with me when Nathan sticks his manicured hand out again.

"Sorry, honey," he says to Mum. "Chloe's on her way up in the lift to collect the ki— I mean, Flo. We've got a meeting with *Hey There!* magazine, remember? I said they could come here and chat now, rather than drag it out and do it later today. Yeah?"

Great. Another chance to read about my mum and her life, rather than actually be part of it.

"Sorry; I promise we'll have longer next time," Mum says, hugging me and kissing me and squeezing me tight before Chloe comes.

All the while she has no idea that I have the urge to grab one of the giant vases of lilies and toss them over the head of the next person who says "Yeah?" to me.

"Hey, ready to go, yeah?" says Chloe, appearing at our table.

It takes all my willpower not to reach out for the nearest vase.

Especially since I can see from the clock on the wall that it's not quite two. From here, Mum said it would be just a short taxi ride to the bus station at Victoria.

That means a couple of things:

1) I'll have to hang about the bus station for nearly an hour before my coach home.
2) My precious "day" with Mum has lasted about three hours.

I'm not a predicted A* student for maths, but even *I* know the arithmetic doesn't add up.

Yeah. . . ?

Sunday 22nd July

"What are you writing?" I ask, looking over the shoulder of the young woman from *Hey There!* magazine.

"Just roughing out my questions for Queenie," the woman answers, tip-tapping on her laptop.

Actually, I already *know* that's what she's doing; I've been silently, sneakily reading them for the last couple of minutes. They're all kind of dumb-sounding, like *Did you enjoy performing at the semi-final last night, in front of all those celebrities?* (to be honest – watching it on TV – me, Freddie, Olive and Wolfie could barely recognize a genuine celebrity in the Z-list audience); *Are you excited about the million-pound record contract you might sign if you win?* (well, duh!); and *Who is your favourite fashion designer?* (Olive? Ha!).

But it's the introduction I've just noticed. . .

Hot favourite Big Dreams *finalist Queenie Rae Brown welcomes us into her wonderfully eclectic living room for our interview today. Tucking her feet under her on the plum velvet sofa, she radiates happiness and confidence.*

There are a couple of glaring errors in that intro.

For a start, Mum doesn't at this minute look either happy or confident. The photographer's lights are so bright they're making her eyes water, and if he's not barking orders at her to twist herself into uncomfortable-yet-photogenic angles, then he's sighing and asking the girl poised with brushes to hurry and touch up Mum's make-up again.

But that's not the *main* problem with what's on the journalist's screen.

We're in a living room all right, but it's not *ours*. This isn't the flat above Armando's. The street outside is *not* Marigold Parade.

"But this is my *friend's* house," I say, nodding over at Alexa, who's standing in the doorway with Polly.

"Artistic licence, honey," the woman smiles up at me insincerely. "Anyway, I'm sure you and your mum will have a place *just* like this when she wins the final. Yeah?"

Gulp.

Everyone thinks Mum's definitely going to win the *Big Dreams* competition.

Every newspaper says so.

The interviewers that Mum has talked to on the twenty radio stations and five TV news shows in the last week say so.

Nathan Reed has said so plenty of times on Twitter (Freddie showed me).

And it's not just them.

Armando is so sure that he's planned a surprise street party for the Sunday after the final. I've tried to tell him that I've no idea when or *if* Mum'll be back, but he's too busy sourcing bunting to listen.

The Ladies are right behind him – they've been practising their own version of "Sugar Sugar" to serenade her with.

And Olive told me yesterday that Bernard's heard the local council are planning an open-top bus ride through our town, with Queenie Rae Brown installed on top, waving to her fans.

It's like everyone's rooting for Mum, and wanting a chunk of her too.

Which doesn't leave a lot for *me*. . .

"Hey!" the photographer barks suddenly, irritated by the ongoing chatter. "How about we get these kids out of here, please?"

Immediately I find myself being shooed away, along with Polly and Alexa, and the living room door is banged firmly in our faces. I wasn't even able to make eye contact with Mum there, 'cause of the reflective lighting umbrellas blocking my view.

"Let's go up to Marley's bedroom – the rest of the place is full of packing boxes," Alexa suggests.

I've sort of drifted back into hanging out with Polly and her friends, ever since Mum hit on the idea of using her dream house in Pear Tree Avenue for the *Hey There!* shoot. (The editor had rejected our flat for being too "intimate". "I think he meant tiny and tatty, Flo!" Mum had laughed down the phone a couple of weeks ago.)

I offered to mention it to Alexa, but the magazine people had already arranged for Mum and the editor to visit the house. Next thing, Alexa's family are being given a large cheque for the use of their house as a location, and Mum gets splashed across page five of the *Daily Mail*, pictured on the steps of this house, with a story saying she's buying the place. (I had a big job trying to assure the Ladies that this latest stupid story wasn't true.)

"God, I can't *wait* to get to our new place," moans Alexa, weaving past a teetering mound of box files on the top landing. "It's so much *bigger* than here."

I smile to myself as I wind upwards behind her and Polly. If only she could see where *I* live, see our little flat and my flatmate Olive. . .

Yes, it's made a nice change and been fun to hang out in Forest Park again. And Freddie hasn't made any more comments about it; maybe he's a bit embarrassed about how over the top his reaction was before. I mean, it's not like I've completely deserted him and Zee, is it? And it's not against the law to have more than two friends, after all. . .

"OK if we come in?" Alexa calls out, rapping at her brother's door.

"Sure," comes a call back, with accompanying strumming of a guitar. "All except *you*, Alexa."

"Very funny, I *don't* think," Alexa snips back, and barges on in anyway.

I follow her and the other girls into the room I imagined would be mine in my alternative fantasy life in Forest Park.

"All right?" Marley drawls as we snake our way in. "What's going on downstairs?"

He's stretched out on his bed, and I'm blown away again by how much he looks like Freddie, only a more perfect, *groomed* version.

"The photographer's a great big nark and told us to get lost, basically," Polly tells him, and settles herself on the window seat, along with Alexa. She's doing a lot of hair-flicking, I notice. Is that for Marley's benefit? Hey, maybe she's into him.

I look around to see where I can sit. There's nowhere obvious, and I'm *just* about to flop down on to the carpet when Marley pulls his legs up and nods to me to sit on the space he's made for me.

"Thanks," I say, noticing Polly suddenly looking a little crushed. Oh, I think I was right; I think she *does* have a thing for Marley.

"Can you believe it? The journalist is going to pretend this is *actually* Queenie and Flo's house!" Alexa fills her brother in.

"Well, it still could be," Polly points out, perking up again. "If Flo's mum wins *Big Dreams*, then she'll be loaded. She could offer more money than the people who're supposed to be buying this place!"

My heart is beating at double its usual speed. It had never occurred to me that the idea of living here was a real possibility.

"That would be amazing!" Alexa exclaims. "We're only moving beside the park so we could all hang out together every weekend."

Now my heart's stopped altogether.

What a weird idea: hanging out with these girls, eating posh cake off antique plates in the Woodlands Café all the time. No more working in Armando's, no more Ladies to wave hello to in the street, no more chemical smells from the dry-cleaner's, or chips from the Beanz Café, no more bumping into Freddie and Zee and Wolfie every five minutes . . . like I say, *weird*.

"So there've been more stories in the papers,

then?" Marley says, directing the comment at me, of course, even though he hasn't used my name, or even bothered to look me in the eye.

More stories. More half-truths and rubbish. More wondering where they're getting all their info from.

"Yes, but my mum has asked the publicity people at *Big Dreams* to make the newspapers stop it," I explain.

"Are you *kidding*?" Marley snorts. "The publicity department will *love* all of that coverage! There's no *way* they'll want that to stop."

My heart lurches as it dawns on me that the *Big Dreams* team maybe aren't exactly on our side.

They might've told the contestants that the show is nothing without their talent, but really, the show itself is what matters to them.

I mean, will *anyone* remember Queenie Rae Brown or any of the others when *next* year's *Big Dreams* rolls round? I mean, I can remember Celeste, who won it last year, but the previous two years . . . nope, not a clue who won then.

"OMG, check this out; there's a really creepy-looking guy on the other side of the road, just sort of staring over at your house, Alexa," says Polly, looking down into the street below.

"Is he paparazzi?" I ask, jumping up off the bed and running over to the window.

"Dunno, but there is something really gross going on with his leg!" Alexa winced. "It's like he's part *robot* or something!"

This I had to see.

Kneeling on the space between Alexa and Polly's legs, I stare down and see a guy in a denim jacket and baggy shorts standing just in front of the Woodlands Café. He's leaning heavily on a crutch. He has some kind of metal contraption around the whole of his left leg. And now I can see what's making Alexa pull a face; it's like metal bolts go directly from the casing *straight* into the man's leg.

With all that going on, I can tell straight away that he's not a photographer from the papers, here to stalk me or my mum.

Then I notice his grey-at-the-sides hair is swooped up into a quiff, and my poor, overstressed heart squeezes so tight I can hardly breathe.

He *is* here to stalk me and my mum.

"I think I know him," I mutter, then thunder off down the stairs to confront my dad. . .

*

I run across the road, get honked at twice, but miraculously manage not to get run over.

It's him.

Of *course* it's him.

He looks exactly like he does in the photo I have in my box under the bed, the one where a tiny me is sitting on his knee. And of course the press printed those pics of him playing guitar, from years ago. . . So he's maybe a little older, and a little stockier, but that man is *definitely* my dad.

Though just to be ultra-sure, I glance down at the hand resting on the crutch. I'm not close enough to see it clearly, but there's something on the inside of his wrist for sure. I'd bet my last tip from Armando's that it's a tattoo of my mum's name.

OK, I've recognized *him*.

But will he recognize *me*?

"@&¥$£*@*!!" he swears, lifting his Ray-Ban sunglasses up to stare at me, this skinny, gawky girl landing in front of him on the pavement. A girl he must've seen all grown up, courtesy of the newspapers and magazines going around. "Flo? Is it *you*?"

So what are you supposed to say to a dad you haven't seen since you were too small to remember him?

Sheer adrenaline sent me flying down here from Marley's room, but I'm now in serious danger of having my voice vanish with shock.

Oh, to be blunt-spoken like Zee, or mouthy-funny like Freddie, and always have something to say.

Hey, that's it; I'll pretend I'm a mixture of my bolshie best friends to get through this, instead of the scaredy mouse I really am.

"Is that any way to greet your long-lost daughter?" I say to my father, putting my hands on my hips to hide how much they're shaking.

I think this is the point on real-life telly shows where relatives separated by distance and years hug it all out.

But not me and Horse.

Apart from that burst of swearing, he seems more speechless than me.

"Want to tell me what you're doing here?" I ask, since that seems to be a pretty obvious question.

"I – I was reading some stuff in the papers about your mum, and I saw she'd been photographed here, saying she was thinking about buying it. I just wanted to look, really," he replied, wiping sweat from his brow. "I didn't know you'd have moved in already. . ."

"We haven't. Either moved in, *or* bought the place," I say, in a voice I hope sounds vaguely bright and careless. (I'm not sure that I want him to know that I care.)

"FLO," a voice suddenly calls out.

"You're wanted," says, er, Dad, and points to the house behind me.

I turn and see Polly, Alexa and Marley leaning out of the upstairs window.

"ARE YOU OK?" Polly yells at me.

"YEAH," I call back, giving her a thumbs up. "HE'S A . . . A FRIEND OF WOLFIE'S!"

I don't know why I said that. All I know is that I want to keep my newfound father to myself for a few minutes at least, till I find out what I feel about this, about him turning up out of the blue.

"Who's Wolfie?" Dad asks.

"Someone Mum hangs out with," I say to this familiar stranger.

Dad's face twitches at that, automatically putting two and two together and guessing – wrongly – that Mum's in love again.

I'm not about to correct that; he hasn't earned honesty and truth.

"Anyway, what's happened to you?" I ask,

pointing at his android leg, all bolts and pins into muscle and skin.

"A lighting rig fell on me during the Crimson Hill sound check at the Astoria," he says. "Smashed my leg up really badly. I've been in hospital for weeks. Just got out this morning."

Hospital.

He's been in hospital.

My thoughts rewind to the backstage door, and the stage crew guy saying Horse wasn't there. He wasn't there 'cause he'd been taken to A&E at our local hospital.

He'd been lying in a curtained-off cubicle, groaning with the pain of his shattered leg, while a thirteen-year-old girl sat in the neighbouring cubicle, having her head examined.

I hadn't been concussed; I really *did* hear the nurse say "Mr Cook" that night.

"Are you OK now?" I ask, feeling so hot that I could self-combust.

"Well," he answers, curling his lip into a wry smile, "still a bit messed up, in quite a few different ways."

"She's inside, you know," I find myself blurting out. "You could see her, if you want."

"Oh . . . oh, *no!*" says Horse, suddenly alarmed. "I didn't expect her – or *you* – to be here. I was just cruising around . . . thinking, remembering."

He's really sweating, I notice, as he nods over to a taxi that's waiting by the kerb, engine running.

"I've got to go," he says, his voice now panicked, his steps stilted and awkward as he lurches his way towards the taxi on his crutch.

What would I say now, if I were a heroine in a movie?

What would the script tell me to do?

"Daddy! Daddy, don't leave me!!"

Yep, that's what I should shout.

But I'm not in a movie.

I'm in a nice-but-normal road in a nice-but-normal town.

I'm a nice-but-normal girl who doesn't know if she hates or loves the man standing in front of her. Who doesn't even know if it's *possible* to love or hate someone who's pretty much a stranger.

And so instead of begging him to stay, I watch as he struggles into the car and feel my heart sinking and my mind going blank, blank, blank. . .

Saturday 28th July

The night Crimson Hill played the Astoria and Olive followed me, she'd planned to make the Espresso Café her surveillance HQ.

She was going to sit here in the window with her Sudoku, keeping a beady eye out for me, making sure I wasn't about to do something stupid that involved my dad.

Boy, she would *kill* me if she knew what I was doing right now. . .

"One latte, one Coke with ice, two blueberry muffins," says the waitress, dunking our order on to the table.

"Thanks!" says Mum.

The waitress is flustered. She's probably been watching Mum on the telly for weeks now, and is slightly bedazzled to have her here, in the flesh, in the Espresso.

"The, er, *Big Dreams* show not on tonight, I noticed?" she says, trying to sound casual, though her hands are shaking.

"Night off – that big annual charity telethon is being shown instead," Mum explains chattily. "Then it's the *Big Dreams* final *next* Saturday."

"Um, OK," the waitress mumbles awkwardly and slopes off.

Till today, I'd never been inside this place; it's normally rammed with mums and buggies.

But luckily there was a spare table at the back when we swung by a few minutes ago, laden down with our shopping bags.

"Are you sure?" Mum had frowned when I suggested it, but I told her I needed the loo and quick, so here we are. "Y'know, me and your dad used to come here when we were young and it was a cool place to hang out. It's changed a lot since then. . ."

I'd pondered that small, unknown piece of family history when I went to the ladies' toilet just now (I stayed in there *just* long enough for it to have seemed like I'd really needed a wee). And on my way back now, I find Mum flicking through a copy of a newspaper, oblivious to the mummy-and-baby brigade staring and whispering all around her.

She's nibbling at her newly manicured nails and I notice that the black varnish has started to chip already.

"Don't read it," I say protectively, slapping my hand over the article she's reading. (I saw it already this morning; Zee showed it to me.)

My own nails have been painted sky blue. The colour is gorgeous but the beautician struggled to make my fingertips look lovely, since lately – due to the stress of keeping secrets – I've bitten them to the quick and picked the rag nails ragged.

"I know, but I can't stop myself," mumbles Mum, gently lifting my hand so she can finish skimming through the story that goes with the "*Queenie's Spending Spree!*" headline. "How do they know this stuff?"

"I'm not sure," I say with a shrug.

But "they" certainly know what Mum – and her credit card – have been up to recently.

"They" know about the new suit she bought for Armando.

The new flat-screen portable TV for Wolfie's back room.

The designer handbag for Olive that's the exact same plum colour as her hair.

The iPhone and iPad for me.

"What's the point? It's not as if buying a few treats is a major news story, is it?" Mum protests.

I don't like to say, and I don't want to seem ungrateful, but it's hardly just a few treats. Mum's spent a *serious* amount of money lately. Even today, there've been the expensive manicures and pedicures at the beauty salon, and the bags at our feet are packed full of two or three hundred pounds' worth of clothes (I lost count after blinking and gulping at the first few price tags).

"So when are you meeting up with the record company again?" I ask.

It might sound like I'm changing the subject, but I'm not really. As soon as Mum signs her contract with them, the debt she's storing up on her credit card won't matter at all.

"Not till early next week," she mutters, still scanning the article. "Apparently they want to make a big thing of it; get photographers and TV cameras in to witness me signing my contract with them."

Huh? *That* sounded slightly weird, and not like Mum at all. Sort of cocky and assured. Was she beginning to believe the hype about her being the favourite to win the competition?

"Anyway, you're right, Flo!" she says suddenly, slapping the newspaper shut and smiling at me, dimples a-go-go. "I should forget this and concentrate on *us*. It's not often I get to have a whole day with you, is it?"

Again, I don't like to contradict her, but – same

as when I went to London – it's not like it's exactly a *whole* day. Mum arrived from London at 11 a.m. and is being picked up in a taxi at 4 p.m. And half of that time she's been chatting and catching up with everyone on Marigold Parade, which hardly counts as just her-and-me time.

And our block of time together now is about to be interrupted in just a few minutes, I realize, taking my phone out of my pocket and leaving it on the table.

The screen shows it's 2.55 p.m.

(Eeek.)

"Go on, have your muffin," says Mum, shoving a plate over towards me. "That's the great thing about not having to worry about money – we don't have to share. You get a whole cake, not just a half."

It's ridiculous, but that makes me feel instantly sad. I *liked* sharing cakes with Mum. I loved our wonky "half-for-you, half-for-me" ritual.

Everything's changing, isn't it?

And it's going to change pretty dramatically in a few minutes, though Mum doesn't know that yet.

I should warn her, shouldn't I?

Tell her I saw Dad the day of the photo shoot.

Tell her I woke up from my shock-stupor and

managed to grab him and get his phone number before he left in his taxi.

Tell her I guilt-tripped him by text-upon-text into seeing us both today (*"You owe us that, Dad – you know you do"*).

Tell her that he suggested this café, because he remembered that there was one opposite the Astoria. (Though now I know it's 'cause it held memories too.)

Tell her that he was hurt pretty badly in that backstage accident and until a week or so ago he'd been at the local hospit—

"Hey, I was thinking," says Mum, interrupting my muddled meanderings. "After the competition finishes, when things calm down, it would be nice if you and Nathan could meet properly."

"So you ARE going out with him!" I blurt.

She's been playing it down for weeks, saying they're just friends, that he's just helping her out.

"Well, maybe. . ." Mum shrugs shyly. "It's early days."

Now I'm furious with her. She's completely spoiled our not-quite-a-whole-day together by mentioning that big-headed fake. He's interested in parading around with Queenie Rae Brown, the potential star, not hanging out with her mousy thirteen-year-old kid.

And another thing. . .

"Well, you won't have *time* to introduce him, will you, Mum?" I hear myself say snippily. "If you win on Saturday, things are *not* going to calm down. You'll be in the studio, recording your album. You'll be getting interviewed by everyone. You'll go away on tour. You'll—"

My rant is cut short by the jangle of my phone.

I look away from Mum's pink-cheeked, stunned expression and stare down at the text message that's just pinged through.

Oh. . .

I crumple inside, and then a tear slides down my nose and plops on to my untouched muffin.

"What?" says Mum.

"Nothing," I say, remembering – even at this moment when disappointment is crushing the breath out of my lungs – that the *Big Dreams* contestants are not to be bothered with bad, sad or unsettling news.

"Doesn't *look* like nothing, Flo Brown!" says Mum, and a set of black-tipped fingers whizz over and steal my phone away.

"No!" I yelp, aware that the whole café is now staring.

Too late; Mum has seen the message.

"Flo?" Mum says, staring straight at me, holding up the phone.

Since it's there in front of my guilty face, I read the message again.

"Sorry Flo-Flo . . . I know I'm a coward, but I can't do it. Sorry. On my way to airport – rejoining band on tour. I do love you. Dad x"

You know something?

I'm sick of being the grown-up.

I'm sick of trying to organize things.

I'm sick of keeping secrets that might hurt people.

For once, I want to act like a sulky, stupid, crushed-with-disappointment kid.

And so I snatch my brand new iPhone from Mum's hand – and drop it *straight* into my Coke. . .

AUGUST

Saturday 4th August

This wasn't what the four of us had expected when we got our backstage wristbands and were led along endless corridors to be here.

Same as all the other contestants, Mum had been told she could have a morale-boosting five-minute visit from a few of her family or best friends before the show – the all-important *Big Dreams* final – started.

Me and Olive, Armando and Wolfie; we'd left the coachload of Marigold Paraders sitting in our appointed row out in the theatre. We'd taken their "good lucks" and the celebratory marigold garland made by Mrs Chowdri and assumed we'd be shuffled into Mum's dressing room and then pretty much hustled straight out again, before we ruined Mum's camera-ready clothes and make-up with our hugs and kisses.

Instead, we've landed in chaos.

"*Don't* panic," Olive orders.

Automatically, we all take a deep breath and concentrate, especially Mum.

Arguing with Olive doesn't do any good; it's always best to go along with whatever she's suggesting.

"What's the problem?" says Chloe from the production team. "Queenie looks amazing!"

Queenie is *crying*.

"She looks like she's going to a fancy dress party, *dear*," Olive growls. "I mean, it's a *great* outfit, if that India girl was aiming to make her look like a Barbie doll crossed with a *clown*."

And with that spiky dollop of sarcasm, Chloe storms out of the dressing room, hot on the heels of India the stylist, plus another member of staff, who left in a strop a minute ago.

("Call yourself a make-up artist?" Olive had snapped at a girl named Mimosa. "A five-year-old in boxing gloves could've done a better job than that!")

"Here, your majesty," says Armando, bumbling over to the table by the mirror, pulling out a tissue from a box and handing it to my mum. "Dry your beautiful eyes."

Wolfie glances sideways at me. If this wasn't an emergency, we might have both burst out laughing at that comment. If the thick crayoned-on blue eyeliner wasn't bad enough, one horrible fake eyelash must've disengaged itself when Mum started crying and is now stuck to her cheek like a runaway spider.

"Why did you let them change you so much, Mum?" I ask her, staring at the frilly-layered, pink chiffon mini-dress, the shiny white knee-high stiletto boots, and – most shockingly of all – her hair.

It was *down*.

Down and teased into girly corkscrew curls.

"They said since it was the final, I needed to have a dramatic new look!" Mum sniffles.

This isn't good. The clock on the wall is ticking; there's not much time. Mum will need a miracle if she's going to be ready to stand in front of an audience of millions very, *very* soon.

A miracle . . . or a fairy godmother.

Make that *two* fairy godmothers.

"Olive, there's a rack of clothes over there; you'll be able to sort Mum out with something, won't you?" I suggest.

"Of course!" Olive replies, already hurrying over. "Armando, you'll fix up her hair, right?"

"Right!" says Armando, jumping to it and examining the brushes and pins and sprays laid out on the table.

"And Mum," I add, spotting some cotton pads and make-up remover and handing them to her, "you *always* know how to do your own face best."

"Thanks, Flo!" Mum sniffles. "Thanks, everyone!"

"Don't thank *me*; I haven't done anything," says Wolfie.

"Oh, trust me, you did," Mum manages a rueful smile. "When you walked in and saw me and swore – it made me realize how *bad* it really was, Wolfie. I mean, I knew it myself, and kept arguing with the stylist and make-up artist, but they wouldn't listen."

"Well, in that case, I'm glad I made you cry!" Wolfie grins at her. "Anything to help, Quee—"

His sentence is interrupted as the door flies open.

It's the production team girl who took us along here a few minutes ago, and she's not alone.

"Queenie! Babe! What's the drama?" asks Nathan Reed, holding his arms out wide. Wow, his teeth are literally outshining his white silk shirt.

"No drama happening here, thanks," Olive says drily. "Queenie just needs some time and she'll be good as new."

The production team person twiddles with her clipboard and says, "The hair and make-up girls—"

"—are *sacked* from this particular job," Olive announces.

"But—"

"But nothing," Olive says firmly to Nathan. "Look, it's like this: if you people want this woman to get up on stage and sing her heart out on your stupid show, you need to leave her with this man and me."

"But you can't—"

"Yes, they *can*," Wolfie says, looming intimidatingly tall over the toothy TV presenter. "Now why don't you leave these people to work their magic, OK?"

And with that, the production girl and Nathan Reed find themselves on the corridor side of the door, as Wolfie firmly closes it in their faces. . .

We squeeze back into our seats just as the act before Mum finishes.

"Where have you been?"

"We were worried!"

"Everything all right?"

"Is Queenie OK?"

The whispered comments and questions; I'm too rattled to figure out who's saying them. It could have been any of the large posse of Ladies, or perhaps someone from Freddie or Zee's family. And it's not just them who came on the Queenie supporters' coach today. There's also Roxanne and Valerie (sadly), lovely Bernard and Philip from the dry-cleaner's, and even David the accountant and Ben, Kenzo and Tim, his student tenants from the flat above (Wolfie pointed out it would be kind of weird to invite the entire street except them).

The Marigold Paraders; we'll be easy to spot from the stage. Armando arranged and paid for a whole bunch of T-shirts to be made up for us all – they say:

**Her Majesty the
QUEENIE!**

We're all wearing them, from muscly huge Wolfie to teeny, tiny baby Roo.

But even with our dumb identikit tops on, we look pretty normal compared to some people in the audience. Someone, somewhere has made up these nasty nylon beehive wigs, and a ton of people have them perched on their heads.

Oh, and Freddie's got one on too, 'cause he just would.

"Are you OK, Flo?" he asks as I squidge past him. The concern in his face doesn't match the toppling mound of fake hair he's wearing, complete with a trashy plastic daisy rammed in the side.

"Everything's cool," I say as I take my seat next to him. "Small technical hitch!"

"Oh, yeah?" he grins at me, knowing I'm joking and that there's a lot more to the story.

But now's not the time to tell him. The bloke on the stage is announcing the end of the latest video montage, and the lights are twirling crazily as we all wait for the five . . . four . . . three . . . two . . . one . . . countdown.

"WELCOME BACK, LADIES AND GENTLEMEN, BOYS AND GIRLS!" Nathan Reed bellows over the crazily screaming crowds.

With a few flaps of his arms, the noise abates.

"So are we ready for our next finalist?"

Roars and cheers.

Arm flapping to quiet everyone.

"Are we ready to hear the sublime voice of this superstar in the making?"

More roars and cheers.

More arm flapping.

"Well, it gives me great pleasure to introduce the one, the only, the divine Miss QUEENIE RAE BROWN! Give it up!!"

Insane roaring and cheering – which fades away as the lights sink down low.

And here she comes, padding on to the stage in the plain gold shift dress that Olive chose for her from the rack. It's simply accessorized with Mum's own wide black cinch belt, black leggings and her black ballet pumps. Her hair is wound up in her trademark beehive, with some orange marigolds from Mrs Chowdri's garland pinned in to the side.

I want to cry, she looks so beautiful.

And I want to cry for upsetting her so much last week. I couldn't stand the shock on her face when I explained that I'd seen Dad, that I'd tried to get them – *us* – together, that he'd let me – *us* – down at the last minute.

She says it's all fine now that we've talked it through and we've got to put it – *Dad* – in the past, but I still feel a little like I'm bruised from the inside out. Does Mum maybe feel the same?

It doesn't look like it right at this second.

She is poised, one hand on her retro mic, her

head dipped, showing off the swoop of black eyeliner she drew on her lids earlier.

And then, as the music swells, Queenie Rae Brown lifts her chin to face the audience.

I think I see her red-lipsticked mouth twitch very slightly with nerves, and go to grip Olive's hand – but she's already reaching for mine. The two Brown girls in the audience, sending out love and support to the lone Brown girl on the stage.

Of course, it's not only *us* who'll be sending out love and support to Mum; it's everyone in this row. Everyone in this theatre. Everyone watching at home. Celebrities who were shown in video clips on previous episodes, sending their best wishes.

Basically, the whole *nation* is waiting breathlessly to be stunned by another of Queenie Rae Brown's amazing, spine-tingling performances.

"*Come on, Mum!*" I whisper under my breath, as I feel Freddie reaching to hold my other hand.

After three minutes of this next song, it'll be roses and cherries and sprinkles-on-top. Isn't that what Mum promised?

And then she opens her perfectly-lipsticked mouth and blasts into her song; "Will You Still Love Me Tomorrow?" by the sixties girl group the Shirelles.

And when I say Mum blasts into her song, I really, literally mean *blasts*.

And honks.

And croaks.

And fades away, as she forgets her words.

For a few seconds, the world stands still, though I can hear the band ploughing hopefully on, willing my mum to cast her nerves aside and launch back into her song.

Instead, Mum lets go of the mic and runs off into the wings.

Frozen as I am, I know something for sure.

In the space of half a verse, Queenie Rae Brown's big dream is over. . .

SEPTEMBER

Tuesday 4th September

I've been doing a lot of flopping lately.

Flopping on my bed, flopping on Zee's bed, flopping on a table at the Beanz Café with Freddie, and now I'm flopped in Wolfie's padded chair.

It's a bit like something you'd sit in while you were at the dentist's, only without a bright light shining in your eyes.

Unless you count the sparkles twinkling off the disco ball that Wolfie's currently attaching to the ceiling. He saw it in the window of the Animal Aid charity shop by the bus station and decided it was the very thing to take his clients' minds off the pain he's inflicting on them.

"So, madam," he says now, glancing down at me from the rickety stepladder. "What can I interest you in today? A tattoo or a piercing?"

"Neither."

I smile, though I'm sighing inside. I'm always sighing inside these days. "But if you've got a suggestion for cheering up Mum, I'll have that!"

"Tell her you'll allow her to have a new tattoo!" Zee suggests with a grin as she sits cross-legged on the floor, holding her baby brother steady. Roo is balancing precariously on his tiptoes, transfixed by the disco ball's glints and glimmers.

"I'm not that desperate!" I joke back, knowing that Wolfie won't take offence.

Actually, I *am* pretty desperate. Mum hasn't left the flat in a month; not since the night of the *Big Dreams* final. While Wolfie and Olive fought their way backstage to rescue Mum after her fateful performance, Armando organized a taxi to take her, Olive and me back home. Meanwhile, the rest of the puzzled and worried Marigold Paraders all piled back in the coach for a sombre return journey.

And since then I've had the weirdest, strangest, saddest summer holidays ever. Mum will only let me and Olive see her and take care of her.

By phone, by email and in person, me and Olive have had to say "no" and "go away" and "thanks but no thanks" in a variety of ways to all sorts of people, from the *Big Dreams* staff to a million radio, TV and newspaper reporters.

Not that it made any difference; of *course* they still printed stories.

"Queenie's Rule Is Over."

"The End Of Queenie's Reign."

"Queenie Loses Her Crown."

"From Queenie To Pauper!"

Most of them were just made up of the "facts": Mum had some kind of nervous wobble/panic attack/breakdown on live TV, and blew her chance of fame.

But some of them – like previous stories – had lots of detail in them that seemed too close to home. "*Queenie – already slender – is losing weight worryingly, says a close friend.*"

Who is this mysterious "close friend"? How do the newspapers know Mum's off her food? They can't see in; knowing the intrusive press interest, Olive made extra-thick net curtains for our flat, and Maureen, Lilian and Mrs Jennings road-tested them and said they definitely couldn't see in to our place from over *their* side of the street.

"*I* know!" says Wolfie, clomping off his ladder now that the job is done and pointing to one of the designs pinned to his wall. "I'll do this on you, Flo.

I mean, *yes*, you're underage to get a tattoo done, but I won't tell if you don't!"

The image is of a red heart with the word "Mum" in the middle in swirly writing.

"Thanks, but I'd rather have hot pins rammed in my eyes," I tell him.

"Could be arranged," he shrugs, nodding over towards his inking drill.

Stupid, spikey black humour; it's the only thing that's kept me going these last few surreal weeks. Freddie, Zee and Wolfie are all great at getting me grinning; they can see when I'm flagging with the effort of looking after Mum. That, and the *guilt* that's weighing me down. Mum keeps saying it was all her own fault; that she let tiredness and homesickness and a lack of confidence trip her up on the night of the final.

But if I hadn't tried to get Dad to meet us, if she hadn't had him on her mind all that week. . .

I just worry that Mum messed up her chance of success because of me and my stupid, secret surprise that had fallen flat – oh, so *flat*.

"Guess I better go," says Zee, scrambling to her feet and scooping up Roo. "Mum's taking me out to buy new school shirts for tomorrow."

School. . . I don't know if I'm looking forward to it or dreading it. It'll be great to be somewhere that isn't Marigold Parade, but I'm not exactly looking forward to the questions or stares that are bound to await me. At least Freddie and Zee will be there to protect me from the worst of it. And although I haven't seen or heard much from Polly or Heidi in the last few weeks 'cause of the school summer holidays, I know I can count on them too.

"And I guess I should go up and check on Mum," I say, pushing myself out of the squashy chair.

"Hold on, Flo," says Wolfie, and strides away from the front of the shop. Out of sight of his clientele, he has been growing several pots of marigolds on the windowsill of his back room, the big Goth softie that he is.

Every day he cuts a golden orange flower and gives it to either me or Olive to present to Mum. It's his way of showing he cares, till she's ready to see him. It's such a sweet gesture it makes me want to hug the great big tattooed lump, but I'm trying to avoid hugs, since I worry they might make me cry and I might never be able to stop.

"He's so cute!" Zee says as she pulls the door

open, ready for us to leave. "Not like some people I could mention. . ."

She's talking about Nathan Reed, of course.

"Will You Still Love Me Tomorrow?" was the song Mum had sung — sort of — on the night of the *Big Dreams* final.

It hadn't been meant as a question directed to him, but if it had, the answer would've been a resounding "no". Nathan Reed didn't love my mother the next day, or any day after her fall from grace. He was never one of those people who persistently rang or emailed. He never contacted her again, and only a week later I saw a magazine in Armando's with an article about Nathan and his new love; some girl who's the hot favourite to win this year's *Britain's Next Top Model* contest.

"FLO!"

Freddie appears on the pavement outside the shop, his floppy hair and apron flying he's been running so fast.

"What is it?" I ask, panic welling in my chest.

"There's a fight. In Armando's. It's all kicking off. We could hear it in the café."

What? I only left there twenty minutes ago. It's been my summer job, and when I've not been looking after Mum or flopping somewhere, I've been keeping sane and earning money by sweeping and making cups of tea while listening to the Ladies sing-songing.

Has there been a bust-up between some of the old girls about what tunes to sing? Or who's going to do the solo? (They're taking their singing very seriously these days.)

"It's Armando," Freddie almost seems to answer me, even though I haven't asked any questions out loud.

With that he's off, with me following – and as we reach the door of the salon, we're just in time to see Roxanne and Valerie storming out, handbags and jackets on their arms. Their faces are flushed, but they have their chins held high and indignant.

They don't even bother to acknowledge me and Freddie. Actually, they might even be deliberately *ignoring* us.

"And I mean it!" Armando is roaring from inside the shop. "You might be my family, but you're FIRED!"

I tentatively step into the salon, and see a sea of bewildered customer faces, some with hair dripping wet, some with heads dipping out from under driers. Mrs Jennings and Maureen, with black hairdressing gowns draped around them, are comforting a red-faced Armando, like two gentle, elderly bats.

"Flo!" he says, his gaze landing on me. "Oh, Flo, you must forgive me."

With that, he drops his head into his hands and sobs.

I glance around madly, hoping someone can tell me what's going on.

They do.

A flurry of Ladies fill me in, line by line.

"He went to see what was taking Roxy and Val so long—"

"—they'd supposedly gone to the kitchen to make tea—"

"—he caught them on speakerphone to some journalist—"

"—turns out they've been selling stories about your mum to the press for *months* now—"

"—conversations your mum has had with Armando—"

"—even things *you've* told him here, Flo, about how Queenie's doing—"

"So it was *them*," Wolfie's voice comes from behind me. "Whenever it was 'a close friend says'. . .."

He tapers off, but I get it now.

"I'm so, *so* sorry, my princess," says Armando, breaking away from his comforting bats and stretching his arms out to me. "Some things my girls heard here; some things I might have told them at home. They are my family; I thought I could trust them!"

"Huh" comes a snort that could only belong to Olive. She must have bustled along here when she heard about the commotion. "You *really* are a very silly old man to think those two shrews of yours could keep anything to themselves, especially gossip about my daughter! They've *always* been jealous of—"

"*Stop*. That's enough."

There's a gasp from all the Ladies. They've seen Mum before I have, since she's right behind me.

They're gasping because they haven't set eyes on her for such a long time, and they have certainly never seen her the way I know she's looking now.

I swivel round and catch sight of Wolfie planting a happy-to-see-you kiss on her cheek.

Next to him, with her make-up-free face, hair hanging in plaits and her too-skinny body hidden beneath an old sweatshirt and jeans, she looks like a little girl lost.

"Are you OK?" I ask, happy to see her outside the prison of our flat, even if the reason for it isn't particularly joyful.

"I'm fine; I just heard the arguing from upstairs," she says.

"Queenie! Your majesty!" Armando calls out, redirecting the hug he'd been aiming at me towards my mother instead. "Please forgive me, and please come work for me again. I can't manage in the salon without you."

Mum's expression softens as she hugs him right back, showing Armando that she isn't angry with him.

"'Welcome home. WEL-come. . .'" Maureen suddenly starts singing. It's a corny, old-fashioned-sounding song I've never heard before, but the other Ladies obviously know it, and join in.

As their voices trill around her, Mum's eyes twinkle with tears and happiness and her face breaks into a smile.

OK, maybe I was wrong; maybe she's not a little girl lost after all.

She might just be a little girl found. . .

Saturday 22nd September

This is supposed to be fun.

"A party," Mum said. "Just a little one, Flo, for all the people who've been there for us both this year."

So our flat is crowded with everyone from Marigold Parade. The retirement houses across the road are empty; the Ladies who live there are all here in our flat, giggling in their glad rags, sipping wine and eating us out of nachos and peanuts at an alarming rate. (Mr Chowdri kindly went to his shop and brought back an emergency six-pack of Monster Munch crisps to refill the bowls.)

Bernard and Philip are in the living room, showing the latest photos of their labradoodle to a politely interested David, the accountant. Ben, Kenzo and Tim – the students who live above David's office – have drunk most of the beer, and are taking turns being a "horsey" for Roo, who's having a fabulous time.

Mrs Chowdri and Angie Rossi are taking the mickey out of Wolfie's attempts to smarten up (he's shaved for once, and they're stroking his stubble-free chin and making jokes about it being as smooth as Roo's bottom).

Mum is tilting her head back and laughing, after

having attempted the jive with Armando, which ended up with him falling backwards over Kenzo when it was his turn to be horsey. (Mr Chowdri and Freddie's dad Mario had to help him up.)

Even Olive seems to be having a good time, but that's probably because she enjoyed seeing Armando make a stupid old fool of himself again.

So OK, quite a lot of the guests at tonight's party *are* having fun.

But there are quite a few who *aren't*.

Example No. 1: Freddie and Zee.

"What are you two doing through here?" I hissed at my best friends a few minutes ago. Last I'd seen of them, they were with Polly and the others in my bedroom, while Marley sat strumming the guitar he'd brought along. I'd left to go in search of snacks, but not finding any in the living room (Mrs Jennings and everyone had made short work of the Monster Munch) I'd come through to the kitchen – and discovered Freddie and Zee sitting on the worktops, sharing a bowl of Hula Hoops.

"Your *other* friends don't seem to be too interested in us," Zee points out.

"Yeah, when you left, they ignored us and carried on talking to each other about people we didn't know from Forest Park," Freddie adds, eating a Hula Hoop off each finger. "And that's *rude*, that is. So we came through here."

You know, I was *so* hoping Freddie had got over this dumb jealousy thing with Polly and her crew. I mean, I'd hardly hung out with them in *weeks*. But they'd been nice to me when the *Big Dreams* stuff was going on, and that counted for something, didn't it? So *that's* why I thought they deserved to be invited to our party.

And here we are now, with Freddie acting all moody and sulky and taking Zee with him. (And Zee doing that intense staring-at-me thing again like she did ages ago, when we made up in my bedroom over ladoos.)

Sadly, it isn't just my supposed best buddies who are having a fun-free time.

Here's Example No. 2: when I gave up on Freddie and Zee and went back towards my bedroom just now, I heard something that made me hesitate outside my bedroom door.

"I didn't think she'd live in such a scuzzy street, did you?" Alexa was saying.

"And this flat's pretty scuzzy too!" I heard Gabrielle add.

"It's so small, isn't it? I couldn't live in a place like this, no way!"

That was Heidi.

"Shhhh, she might hear!"

That was Polly. It might have sounded like she was on my side, only she was giggling.

So now that I have *two* sets of friends having a lousy time, it means *I'm* not exactly feeling in a party mood any more.

Though I wasn't exactly feeling in a party mood before anyone even came, to be honest.

Mainly because of what I'd found in the cabinet drawer when I was searching for cocktail sticks for the sausages. . .

With a sigh, I turn away and quietly open the flat door opposite, and pad my way down the steps. Sitting in the dark stairwell, I rest my head on the wall and feel a breeze blowing in under the slight gap at the bottom of the door to the street.

It feels cool, but I'm burning up with misery at what I've just heard and the stress of discovering yet *another* parental secret.

"Is it OK if I join you?" says a boy's voice that I don't at first recognize. I blink up, thinking it might be one of the students.

"Oh, sure," I mumble, surprised to see Marley.

"You all right?" he asks, settling down beside me.

I don't really *get* this boy.

I mean, he's never acted like he's vaguely interested in me whenever we've met, yet he let me know about the story in the paper.

I don't really know why he's come along with the girls tonight. But now he's sitting here, I feel sort of glad he did. . .

"No, I'm not all right," I answer him, honestly.

"Want to tell me about it?"

"No," I say.

Flattered as I (weirdly) am, I'm not about to tell Marley that I heard his sister and the other girls bitching about me just now, and there's certainly no *way* I'm going to splurge about all those bank and credit card demands I found in the drawer, threatening Mum if she doesn't pay her debts soon.

Still, my bluntness has an unexpected effect on Marley; he bursts out laughing. Which makes *me* laugh, in spite of myself.

As our joint laughter slips softly into giggles, out of the corner of my eye I'm aware of a shadow passing over the light haloed in the doorway to the flat.

I go to turn around, to look up and see who it is, but then I feel a hand gently touch my face.

And lips suddenly, softly kissing mine.

I'm *totally* confused.

But I had no idea being confused felt this good. . .

OCTOBER

Wednesday 17th October

All day, there have been whisperings.

All day.

"What's going on?" I ask Freddie, as me, him and Zee head towards the school gates and the bus stop beyond.

I'm asking because I've spotted another two girls across the playground staring at their phones and then staring at me.

Freddie answers in true Freddie style.

"Stuff 'em," he says, then throws his scrawny arms wide and launches into a typically high-voiced rendition of an old Eliza Doolittle track that was a big hit; the one about ignoring "the whisperers". I can't remember the name of it.

Zee tries to join in with the cute "Tweet tweet!" chorus, but her husky voice doesn't quite cut it for the sweetness of the song.

Or maybe it's just me; nothing sounds right today. I'm too aware of being talked about, sniggered at. I thought all this had stopped weeks ago. The first few days of term, it was pretty inevitable that people would be gossiping about me, gossiping about what had happened with Mum.

But then – thankfully – it just sort of petered out. So did the press interest; the papers and magazines were now all a-twitter over the boy band who went on to win *Big Dreams*. It turns out that the cute Asian one called Kal is now dating the model that Nathan Reed had been seeing. There was a whole bunch of photos of Kal and Nathan having a punch-up in nightclub a couple of weeks back. After what Mum has been through, I don't usually look at that gossipy paparazzi stuff any more, but I have to admit I peeked, just so I could enjoy the sight of Nathan Reed looking like a desperate plonker.

Great; now Polly and Heidi are staring over.

I'm so glad school's finished for the day 'cause I can't take much more of this.

The two girls are saying something to each other. Polly isn't looking very pleased. Heidi is shrugging – and now walking away from her friend towards me, Freddie and Zee.

"Run! It's the enemy!" Freddie jokes. "Retreat, retreat!"

He ducks behind a bush, pretending to quiver with fear.

Heidi doesn't take any notice of him, and just directs a small, shy smile my way.

"Hey, Flo – I know things have been a bit weird lately," she begins with an apologetic shrug of her shoulders.

"You can say *that* again," growls Zee, sounding like a thirteen-year-old version of Olive.

Heidi's not kidding. It's been *extremely* weird since the night of the party. One minute, I was kissing Marley (except it was more that *he* was kissing *me*, and I wasn't exactly stopping him) and the next the blinding stairwell light was flicked on and a steely-faced Alexa stormed past her twin brother and me, followed by tearful-looking Polly and the others.

"Huh?" I muttered, as the street door banged shut behind them.

Marley swooped a hand through his hair and gave me a wry smile. "Polly kind of *likes* me, and so my sister thinks I should ask her out. But there's no *way* I'm going to do anything just 'cause *Alexa* wants me to."

Then Marley said he guessed he should go. He collected his guitar and left, though he stopped just as he was leaving and said he'd text me sometime. (Yay!)

Polly and Heidi stopped talking to me at school after that. Maybe they think me and Marley are a big thing now. Maybe they think we've been seeing each other every single day; me staring into his pale blue eyes while he serenades me on his guitar. Instead, he's texted me just once to say his family are in the middle of moving from their *old* ginormous house in Pear Tree Avenue to their new, even *more* ginormous house by the park, and that I should come on over when they're settled.

I felt a ripple of excitement when I read that, and then a stomach lurch of dread when I imagined Alexa's face if I rang the bell and she found me on her doorstep.

As usual, I've got myself tangled in another secret, of course. Freddie and Zee; they don't know about me and Marley, about the kiss. They think Polly and everyone stomped off from the party because they are a) snobs and didn't want to hang out in "scuzzy" Marigold Parade, and b) not interested in me now that my mum is just an eccentric-looking hairdresser in an old-lady salon instead of a potential superstar.

I hate to admit it, but since the party, I've been thinking that Freddie and Zee have a point. Well, *two* points.

Marley's not like that, though. He was nice to me (*very* nice) *after* the whole mess of the *Big Dreams* show, so he's obviously isn't impressed by celebrity. I wish I could tell them that, but I'm not sure they'd listen.

"The thing is," Heidi continues, "there's something I need to tell you. Unless . . . unless you've seen it already?"

I look at her blankly. She immediately realizes that I really *don't* know a thing about whatever it is that everyone else seems to.

"So – what's up?" Zee steps in and asks on my behalf. Out of the corner of my eye I see Freddie hurrying over, alert to trouble.

"It's her dad," says Heidi, her expression showing genuine concern as she turns from Zee to me. "It's all over Facebook, Flo. And here; there's a link to the actual newspaper article."

My heart sinks. My whole life – or weird, twisted versions of it – have been appearing in print for months. I'd hoped it would finally stop now that interest in Mum has waned.

But this; this has something to do with *Dad*? Have Roxanne and Valerie been up to their old tricks again?

Heidi holds up her phone longways for me and I glimpse the headline: "*Queenie's Sad Ex Opens His Heart*".

Oh, no.

No.

Horse has sold *his* story?!

"Sorry; I know it's rubbish," Heidi says softly, rubbing my arm. "I just thought it wasn't fair if you didn't know."

Do I scream? Throw up? Run? Right this second I could do all three – but I go for the running option.

Some people on the pavement yell at me as I push past them, but I don't care 'cause now I'm on the bus that I just spotted, leaping on *right* before its doors shut reassuringly behind me. I *have* to get back home, get back to Marigold Parade and Mum as soon as I can.

It's only as the first shuddering tears stream down my face that I realize I left Freddie and Zee behind.

*

I'm hyperventilating, while holding a mug that says "Keep Calm and Carry On."

I'm sitting in an office I've never been in before, with a man I've hardly ever spoken to.

"Hmm, I think getting scalded is only going to *add* to your troubles today," says David the accountant, noticing my violently trembling hands and taking my sugary tea away from me.

The newspaper is open on his desk; he'd already been reading it, so I didn't exactly have to explain what was bothering me when he rescued me.

Yes, he rescued me.

I'd come hurtling off the bus, across Grey Street and into Marigold Parade to find it ominously deserted.

Back in five minutes said the sign on Armando's door.

Back soon said the Post-it in the Beanz Café window.

It was the same story in the Chowdris', and I guessed that meant I'd find a similar message at D.B. Gregory Accountants, Marigold Dry-Cleaner's and The Tattoo Den.

And all the shop owners and customers . . . had they been abducted by aliens?

No – I saw that the door of the empty shop was open; heard lots of laughter and clapping coming from inside. My frazzled brain couldn't figure out what was going on. I mean, I knew Armando was having the flat upstairs renovated so he could move in. (He'd put his big house by the tennis courts up for sale; he was planning on splitting the proceeds with Valerie and Roxanne, so all three of them could have their own flats.)

And there was *more* gossip; Bernard from the dry-cleaner's said he'd heard Roxanne and Valerie had opened their own salon in Forest Park, of all places. Probably the money they'd made from the newspapers had helped with that. . .

But I was too much of a mess to go and find out what the sudden celebrations in the shop were all about.

Hoping Mum might for some reason be upstairs in the flat, I tried to put my key in the lock – but my hand was shaking so much I couldn't do it. That's when David, who'd been finishing a phone call before joining the empty-shop-party, came out of his office and spotted the trembling, sobbing mess of a girl that was me.

He'd hurried me past the crammed-with-people

empty shop (all backs were turned to the door, so no one saw), hustled me into his quiet office, and gently poured me into a chair before my jelly legs collapsed.

"I'm guessing *this* is the problem?" he'd said, pointing to the newspaper before giving me the tea – then taking it right back from me again.

And here we are now.

With the Keep Calm mug obliterating Dad's face, I'm glad to see.

"Me and Queenie were a dream team," says Horse, his eyes misting over. "We had it all; each other, our little daughter, our band. And then I blew it. I got the offer to work with Crimson Hill, and I left. I left them. I convinced myself that Queenie was so angry with me that she didn't want to know any more. But lately, when I was in hospital, I had time to think . . . and I think I might have got that all wrong."

Yeah, so you only just worked that out?! I'd yelled silently when I'd read that on my phone on the bus.

There'd been more quotes from my dad along those lines. Then there'd been a whole section about Olive; how he felt she'd turned Queenie against him, because she was so bitter about her *own* life.

It was *that* bit that had upset me the most. To

suddenly find out a chunk of my family's story like this, along with a few million strangers.

"Nobody told me," I sniffle, rubbing my dripping nose with one hand and tapping the column where Dad had moaned about my gran.

David leans over and scans the words. "You didn't know that Olive used to be a singer?"

"That – among other stuff!" I sniffle some more, and gratefully take the tissue David is now passing me.

Brutally honest, plain-speaking Olive; sure, she'd told me she was a humble seamstress in a fancy club. She'd brought up my mum on her own, after she'd divorced her no-good husband. Now – according to Dad and this newspaper – it turns out that Olive was originally a singer at the club, with top billing. The owner, Vince Chesser, wooed her, married her, then ran off to Marbella with another singer and was rumoured to have opened a club there.

In those days, singers in clubs had to be glamorous and gorgeous. But my deserted gran was heavily pregnant and now poor, and had to reinvent herself as a behind-the-scenes helper – a seamstress in Olive's case – just to get by.

"And look; my dad says here that Olive never got round to divorcing this Vince bloke, 'cause she didn't know where to find him and never wanted contact with him anyway."

"I guess Olive must have been very angry, never mind hurt and disappointed," says David. "And sometimes people deal with that sort of thing by blanking out the bad bits of their lives."

How funny. Olive hates Horse, but they have something in common; Dad's obviously a world-class expert at blanking out bits of his life. Even if those bits contain *me*.

Except Dad seems to have suddenly changed his mind about keeping things to himself. Why did he do that? Was it the money? Didn't he earn enough working for a famous rock band?

"But don't you see?" I say to David, going back to jabbing pages four and five of this lousy newspaper with my finger. "It means my gran's name is actually Olive *Chesser*. She always said we're the three Brown Girls, but we're only *two*. Me and *Mum*."

"Yes, but I suppose she never actually meant to—"

"And what's *this* bit about?" I say, unstoppable

now that my breathing's become more normal. "What does Dad mean, 'Our band'? *Dad* was in a band. Mum used to watch him play."

"Well, at *first*," says David. "She watched him and the other guys when they did gigs at the Espresso Café on the high street. It had a stage in the corner at the back in those days."

Huh? How does David B. Gregory the accountant know all this?

"Then I remember this one time she got up and sang with them," he continues, "and everyone went *wild*. After that the band changed their name to Queenie's Boys and played these crazy versions of old rock 'n' roll songs, plus some stuff of their own. I remember she wrote this really great sort of skiffle-sounding song called 'Roses and Cherries'."

With sugar sprinkles on top. . .

I've stopped breathing altogether. I'm now sitting stock-still, staring at David B. Gregory the accountant, who seems to know a *lot* more than is written in the newspaper.

"Hold on," I interrupt him. "How – I mean, what exactly. . ."

David shuffles a bit and then does something unexpected. He pushes his shirt sleeve high up, past his elbow. And there at the top of his arm is something *very* unexpected indeed.

"You have a *tattoo*?" I squeak.

It's the letters Q.B., with a tiny crown on top, and tiny roses for the full stops.

"Stands for Queenie's Boys. It was the logo on their drum kit. I was just a kid, only maybe four or five years older than you, really, but I was a *huge* fan of the band. You can imagine it was a pretty big shock for me when I saw your mum – and you, of course – move in down the street one day."

Information overload, information overload, information overload. . .

"I knew she liked to sing," I finally mumble. "I just thought she did it in her school choir, and for fun, with Dad, at home or something. She's never told me she'd been in a band *with* him."

"It's maybe a lot like Olive's story," David says with a shrug. "Queenie's Boys got a support slot with some band at the Astoria Theatre one night. It was really exciting; the *Herald* reported that they'd got spotted by some agent, and that it could be the start of something big. Then your dad got the offer of touring with Crimson Hill, and he took it. And that was the end of her dreams, I guess."

Wow. It happened to her *twice* then. No wonder my mum went into self-imposed hibernation after the *Big Dreams* final. She saw history repeating itself; a second time that success had vanished from under her feet.

And while I'm thinking about it, *boy*, could she and Olive pick the rubbish men in their lives. (*Please* let me not have inherited that talent from them.)

I find myself suddenly looking at this gentle, quiet man now, and bizarrely feel like I can trust him, since he's *sort* of known my mum – even from a distance – for important chunks of her life.

Or maybe it's just the fact that he's an accountant. The thing is, in the midst of this mess, I've remembered that there's a really HUGE mess that needs sorting out.

A HUGE mess that Mum promised she'll fix when I confronted her after our party. But since when can I rely on my mother to act like a grown-up?

"She owes lots of money. I mean *lots*," I blurt out to David. "She got a bunch of credit cards and store cards, 'cause *everyone* was telling her she was going to win the competition and get a *huge* record deal, and now I'm worried that she's going to end up in real trouble or even in *prison* and . . . and . . . I'll end up completely *parentless*, in the care of someone called Mrs Chesser!"

"Nope! Stop right there, Flo – I've had a couple of meetings with your mum already. Wolfie told her to come see me," says David.

"He did?"

"Yes. And I know I'm blowing client confidentiality here, but just so you don't worry, I've helped Queenie consolidate her debts into one low-interest loan, and although it means her financial status will be compromised, it *is* manageable."

I blink a bit before I speak. "I have no idea what you just said, apart from the bit about not worrying."

"Well," smiles David. "That'll do, won't it, Flo?"

I nod. I smile. I feel a bunch of muscles relaxing for the first time in quite a while.

"Now, how are you feeling?" David smiles, running a hand through his sandy hair and leaving it sticking out at all angles. "Are you up to going next door?"

"Well, yes, I think so. But what exactly is happening in there?"

The last time we'd all been in the empty shop unit was for the party to celebrate Queenie getting through to the Manor House stage of the *Big Dreams* competition. I couldn't imagine what had got the whole street in there *this* time.

"Well, you know how Queenie's been singing with Armando's customers?" says David, going over to the door and holding it open for me.

As I get up from my seat I give a "yes" sort of shrug. In the month where Mum had been hiding out in our flat, she'd loved listening to the muffled sing-songs of the Ladies drifting up from the salon.

She loved it even *more* when she started back at work; turning simple wash-and-blow-dries into coaching sessions on how to harmonize.

"Well, Armando has offered your mum the empty unit next door – as a choir rehearsal space."

"He did?" I say, the cool air of the street feeling good on my hot cheeks.

This shy guy David, good old Wolfie and dependable Armando . . . how lucky was my mum to have these people looking out for her? And now, in turn, she's looking out for the Ladies, giving them something to look forward to every week, something that'll get them out of their lonely little houses.

"Well, although there's no financial gain to be had, Armando saw this 'free lease' situation as an opportunity to maintain the property, instead of it lying empty and decaying."

I stare at the back of David's head as he locks the office door.

What he just said; Armando would *never* have come out with anything that technical.

"Did you suggest that to him?" I ask, as a certain truth dawns on me.

David glances up at me sheepishly. "Um, *maybe* I said something along those lines."

"OK. . . And just wondering; does Mum remember you from the days of the band?" I can't help but ask.

"Um, no; I was a bit younger than Queenie and your dad. I wouldn't really have been on her radar. And I've never mentioned it to her all these years later because it would've just been a bit cringey to admit that *I* was the kid who was always whooping and singing along at the front whenever they played."

As we turn to walk to the up-till-now-empty shop next door, I can't help asking one more question.

"Does she know about—"

"No!" David laughs nervously, slapping a hand on his upper arm, right where the Q.B. tattoo is hidden under his shirt sleeve. "But how about we don't mention that for now? Just let Queenie enjoy the moment?"

I smile and nod.

He doesn't know me well enough to know I'm a bit of an expert at keeping secrets.

And all these years that he was quietly working away in his office down the Parade, who knew that D.B. Gregory, Accountant, was as madly in love with Mum as Wolfie. . .?

NOVEMBER

Friday 2nd November

"I thought bunting," says Mum, sweeping her arms up at the blank space in front of her.

"Oh, *no*," says Olive, folding her arms across her chest and crinkling her nose in distaste.

Freddie, me and Zee exchange grins and glances.

We've spent the autumn half-term painting the not-empty-shop clean and white, ready for Queenie's Choir to start their rehearsals.

The Ladies are beside themselves; two nights a week and every Sunday morning, they can be here, singing their hearts out. And they won't disturb the tenant in the flat directly upstairs: Armando – newly moved in – is dying to accompany them on his keyboard. (Roxanne and Valerie used to banish *it* and *him* to the garage in the big house by the tennis courts.)

"Well, fairy lights, then," says Mum.

Olive makes a face like Mum's suggested smearing the walls with porridge and ketchup.

"Well, what decorating ideas have *you* got, Mrs Chesser?" I ask, and hear Freddie snort into his paint-splattered T-shirt.

"*Flo*," says Olive, staring at me ominously over her glasses.

Ha – it's my one weapon against Olive. Just to get her back for not telling me her whole story and letting me read it in a tatty newspaper. As for Mum, *her* punishment for not telling me about her earlier singing aspirations was this: I got a fake "I Love Mum" tattoo from Claire's Accessories and pretended for about three days that it was real. (Wolfie played along, bless him, even when Mum went crazy at him for being so irresponsible.)

Though I suppose – once I thought about it – I *did* understand Mum and Olive's explanation.

"Flo-Flo . . . I'm sorry you had to read all this in the paper. But me and Queenie would have told you everything *eventually*," Olive had said that night, at the kitchen table in our flat, after the celebration in the empty shop along the Parade. "The thing is, you're only just thirteen, and we decided – Queenie and I – that you'd had MORE than enough drama in your life already, what with that disaster of a father of yours, without hearing about *our* various disas— OW!"

That was when Mum gave *over*-plain-speaking Olive a shut-up whack in the arm for describing Horse as a disaster. But you know what? After that tell-all story in the paper, after that no-show meet-up in the Espresso Café, after having bailed out on me and Mum way back when I was small. . . I don't think *Olive* was the one who deserved to be whacked – *hard* – on the arm.

For a long time, I hadn't been able to figure out how I felt about my dad, but now I knew for sure that it was a lot, *lot* closer to hate than love.

"If you're looking for something to brighten the place up, Queenie, how about using those photos Flo's got on her phone?" Freddie suggests. "You know; the ones of the marigolds in little glasses and mugs?"

He's talking about the photos I took of the flowers Wolfie sent up to our flat, day by day, when Mum was going through her post-*Big Dreams* bad time. I wasn't sure Mum would want to be reminded of that. . .

"Oh, I love that idea, Freddie!" Mum says now.

"Those would look great in frames, all around the walls."

Good; Mum sounds like she's on a high. And it's not just because this space is nearly finished, it's because Queenie's Choir have their first gig booked already – at the beginning of December, at the Town Hall Square, to celebrate the annual Christmas Market setting up.

"Flo could take the photos to the printers, get them blown up huge!" Freddie says enthusiastically.

"Too expensive," I say, more realistically. "But I could always get them done A3 size on David's colour photocopier next door. . ."

Of *course* David wouldn't mind that. After getting to know him and his secret band-fan past, I was pretty sure David would *never* mind anything that would help Queenie out.

"And there are big frames down at the 99p Store by the bus station," says Olive, suddenly into the idea. "I could pop along and get some now."

She shrugs her way into her cosy winter coat and is gone.

"And I could ask my mum to make good-luck marigold garlands for the door," Zee suggests.

Me, Mum, Freddie and Zee . . . we're all smiling,

sure this is a fantastic theme for the Queenie's Choir rehearsal room.

And then my mobile goes and spoils everything.

"*Long time no see*," says the text.

From Marley.

Who I've heard nothing from in *weeks*.

A boy who veers from ignoring me to caring to kissing to ignoring me again. And then up he pops. I should be mad, but I'm suddenly stupidly giddy and happy.

"Who's that?" asks Freddie, as if he's suddenly developed psychic powers to read my thoughts, or X-ray vision to read my texts.

His face; he looks like a bunny caught in the headlights, just about to be squished in the road.

I dunno. This whole year . . . just when things seem to be going right, they go completely wrong again. I mean, I should be pleased to hear from Marley again, but if it means one of my two best friends is going to go severely weird on me, then—

Oh.

When Freddie said, "Who's that?", he wasn't looking at me, or my phone.

He was looking *outside*.

Looking outside at someone who I can now see standing on the pavement, the sleety rain landing on the shoulders of his scrubby-green parka.

And on his greying quiff. . .

Poor Angie Rossi.

Freddie's mum rushes out to our table in the Beanz Café with full mugs of tea in her hands, scalding herself rotten in her haste.

"There! Enjoy!" she squeaks, before hurrying away to the kitchen, where she'll no doubt run her hands under the cold tap to counteract the burns, and try her best – alongside Freddie and his dad Mario – *not* to listen in to what me, Mum and Horse are saying.

"So. . ." says Mum, since the silence is over-whelming.

I'm proud of her; she is pretty calm on the outside, even if she's maybe not feeling that way on the inside.

Horse fidgets with his walking stick, which I guess is an improvement on the crutches. He's wearing normal jeans, with no sign of the scary robo-pins and screws that had held his leg together last time I saw him.

"Yeah. . ." Horse mutters, scratching self-consciously at his long sideburns.

I'm going to stay out of this.

I know I'm probably more grown-up and mature than both my mum and dad (definitely my dad!) put together, but this is *their* moment. Their moment to clear the air, after eleven long, sad, muddled years.

Anyway, today, sitting here between them, I suddenly feel more like the shy toddler I was the last time we were a "family".

"What are you doing here, Horse?" Mum says.

"You mean, why am I *able* to be here, or why have I *come* here?" he checks hesitantly.

"Both," she replies coolly.

"Well, Crimson Hill are back here in the UK for a couple of days to go to some music magazine award ceremony, so I thought I'd hitch a lift on the private jet and. . ."

Horse fidgets with his stick and rubs a hand through his quiff as Mum and me wait for his explanation.

". . .and say I am sorry. *So* sorry," he carries on, as if every word is as painful as his once-smashed leg. "OK, so here's what happened. This guy in Berlin; he said he was a *huge* Crimson Hill fan and wanted to talk to me after the show about the amps they use, technical stuff like that. So he took me out for a beer. And then several – OK, way, *way* too many – beers later, he's got me taking about *you*, Queenie, and us and everything. Cross my heart, I really didn't know he was a journalist. Honest and true."

So Dad was duped.

He didn't do it to be mean, he didn't do it for money (unlike Valerie and Roxanne). He did it because he was gullible and drunk and—

"Stupid," he adds out loud now. "That's me. . . Stupid and useless in so, so, *so* many ways."

If someone made a perfect, life-sized origami man, then crumpled it up in their hands – that would be what my dad looks like right now.

"Well, you're right there," says Mum with a wry smile. "Stupid enough to break a promise you made to your daughter too. Why did you let her down that day? Why did you promise her you'd meet us in the Espresso and then not turn up?"

Under the table, we are holding hands, her finger circling my palm. For once, she feels really and truly like the grown-up out of the two of us. And I really like that.

"I decided you'd think I was just getting in

touch 'cause you were doing so well in that contest, Queenie," says Horse. "You, Olive, Flo . . . everyone would've thought I was trying to cash in."

As he speaks, Dad rubs the thumb of one hand on the "Queenie Forever" tattoo on his wrist.

In that instant, I know that he is genuinely useless, genuinely stupid, and genuinely *genuine*.

In fact, in his own pathetic way, Horse beats Nathan Reed hands down. He's honest about himself and his 0/10 rating as a partner and father. But at least he didn't ever want to make it seem like he was getting in touch with me or Mum for selfish reasons.

"Look, I didn't want to come here to make your lives more complicated," he says now, shuffling to his feet and trying to find some change in his pockets to pay for the undrunk teas. "I just needed to let you know what had really happened with that newspaper story. I probably shouldn't have come at all. . ."

Mum slides her free hand – the one not holding mine – over his. For a second, unseen, we are joined.

"I'm glad you did," she says softly. "Thanks, Horse. And stay in touch from time to time, yeah?"

"I will," he promises, limping slightly towards the door of the café. "But, hey – can I ask a question?"

The wintry afternoon light makes a silhouette of him and his quiff.

"Sure," says Mum, smiling kindly at him.

"Does Olive want to kill me?"

"Oh, *yes*!" I suddenly yelp, a smile breaking out on my face in spite of the oddness, the slight sadness of the moment. "She'll tear your head off if she catches you here!"

"Better run, then!" Dad jokes wryly, waving his walking stick. "I'll drop you guys a line from Australia soon, if that's all right, then?"

"Flo?" says Mum, turning to me.

I look at her, and then shyly at my nervous, useless and stupid dad, who I don't hate, and don't love, but think I might come to *like*, just a little bit.

"It's all right," I smile and nod.

And he's gone.

There's nothing left of my mostly invisible dad . . . except for a scribble I see on a serviette beside his undrunk mug of tea – an email address.

An email address where I can contact Horse, if I ever want to.

And if that's OK with Mum, it might feel OK to do.

"How are you feeling, Flo?" Mum asks me now,

her eyes sparkling green, her smile wide and ruby-red.

"Not sure," I say with a wobbly smile in return, and let my head drop on to the sprig of red flowers wending down from her shoulder.

"Well, it's not quite roses and cherries, but it's a start, yeah?" she murmurs, wrapping me up in a hug.

You know, it actually *does* feel like it might be the start of something.

Seeing Dad, hearing his sorries; it's as if a shadow of sadness has finally lifted away from Mum, from both of us.

Letting myself relax, I snuggle into her arms, glad that Queenie is my mother, glad that I'm her little girl. . .

DECEMBER

Saturday 1st December

"Can we go now?" I ask.

"In a minute," says Marley, his sun-kissed hair flopping over his guitar.

He's playing some track by Elbow. I can't remember the name and I don't like to ask, in case he thinks I'm dumb.

I hide my anxious sigh, and check my watch. Again.

There's no point rushing Marley when he's playing his guitar, same as there's no point arguing with Olive when she's decided she's right. So I drum my fingers and glance around the vast living room, at the squashy sofas, the mini grand piano, the canvas picture on the wall. It's one of those "fun" family photo portraits, with Marley and Alexa's parents laughing while Marley cradles his precious guitar and his twin swooshes her long hair prettily.

Alexa didn't look that pretty when she answered the door to me an hour ago.

"He's through there," she'd said flatly, pointing to the living room, then disappearing up the stairs of her huge new house.

To be honest, I wasn't any more pleased than *she* was to be here. I'd seen Marley four times in the last month; three times I'd come to his, and three times I'd had to put up with Alexa's disapproving glower. The one other time, he suggested meeting at the Woodlands Café, which would've been OK if Alexa, Polly, Heidi and Gabrielle hadn't been in there too. (Heidi gave me a tiny smile hello, unseen by her friends, but it only made me feel a *speck* less uncomfortable.)

Today, I'd hoped Marley would've come to mine, since Marigold Parade is a lot closer to the Town Hall Square than *his* house is. But when we talked on the phone earlier, Marley said he had stuff to do . . . and why didn't I come to his first?

So I came.

So this stuff he had to do; it just seems to have involved playing endless Elbow songs.

DRRRRRRRRRRRRR-DRRRRRRRRRRRRR.

I put my mobile on vibrate when I first got here, so it wouldn't disturb Marley playing.

"*Where ARE you?!*" says the text.

"*I'm on my way,*" I reply to Freddie's message.

"*Everyone's here. Choir. Mayor. BUT NOT YOU!*"

The knot tightens in my tummy; it's Mum's big day . . . we really *have* to get going.

"Listen – I'm out of here," I tell Marley, gathering up my stuff. "You can come along later, if you like."

Marley is the most beautiful boy I've ever seen. He plays guitar like he should be in a band. When he kisses me, it's like my insides are made of marshmallow and stardust.

But today isn't about him.

It's about Queenie Rae Brown, who I am *so* proud of.

"Jeez, I'm coming, I'm *coming!*" he laughs at me, lazily swinging his guitar to one side and propping it up against the wall. "Now where did I put my trainers. . ."

This Saturday, just this once, just for a couple of hours, Marigold Parade is shut.

The neat little houses across from the shops are empty, all their occupants now up on the stage erected outside the Town Hall.

The Marigold Parade shops have their *Closed* signs turned round, since everyone who works in them is here to cheer on Queenie's Choir on this bright but freezing wintry morning.

I wriggle through the crowd to the front, where I can see Freddie clapping his hands above his head and singing along as the choir (average age seventy) blast out Beyonce's "Single Ladies".

"Hey, Flo! Join in!" Freddie shouts and beams when he sees me – then turns away as soon as he spots Marley.

Zee – bouncing Roo in her arms – widens her eyes at me. There's an unspoken "Where have you been?" hanging in the air.

There's no mistaking it; she's angry with me.

"Have I missed much?" I ask her nervously.

"The mayor introduced the choir, and they've already done 'Sugar, Sugar', so yes."

Zee throws a dark look behind me at Marley, who's idly glancing at his mobile.

I feel a huge surge of disappointment and guilt. I should've just left; if I hadn't waited around for the ten minutes it took Marley to find his Vans, then I'd have made it for the start of the concert.

"Do you think Mum noticed I wasn't here?" I ask

Zee as I glance up at Queenie. She and her dark beehive are in the middle of a sea of white-haired women, all swaying as they sing along to Armando's accompanying keyboard.

"Luckily for you, she's been too busy to notice," says Zee drily. "But plenty of *other* people missed you."

OK, so she means Olive, right?

'Cause I can see the one plum-haired person in the choir gazing right at me now. She's raising her eyebrows above her glasses. That's code for "So, you've finally decided to grace us with your presence, have you, madam?"

Unlike Freddie, Marley is *not* exempt from her men-hating list. Which isn't fair; she hasn't even met him properly. "Hmm, I know *his* kind," she'd muttered darkly when I came home later than I'd promised last week. "And if Freddie doesn't like him, that's good enough for me. . ."

Well, Freddie and Zee are *never* going to like Marley, since they bundle him up in their minds with Polly and Alexa and the Forest Park crew, and think of them *all* as snobs and fakes.

It's maddening, it really is. I step to one side and motion Marley to come and shuffle in beside me, so

Olive and Freddie and Zee can see how supportive he is.

"No *way*!" he laughs at me, at the same time as his fingers fly across the keypad of his phone.

I frown, and motion him again.

"Are you kidding, Flo?!" he says in my ear. "*I'm* not standing right at the front. Not at something as corny as this!"

Clunk.

That's the sound of a big fat realization hitting me in the face.

"Marley," I say. "Can I ask you something?"

"Yeah," he answers, his gaze more on his phone than on me.

"Why did you text me that first time? When you let me know about that story in the *Sun*?"

Marley looks up at me, confused now, as if that was such a non-event that it's hard to remember it at all.

"Oh, yeah, that . . . my sister wanted to tell you but I thought it would be kind of fun to bug Alexa and get in there first. Ha!"

Time is suspended for a second.

On one side of me, Zee is jiggling her giggling baby brother in time to the music.

On the other, Freddie is crooning along in his highest voice, his arms waving unselfconsciously in the air.

And just behind me is this intensely gorgeous boy with grey-blue eyes. Eyes that I'm staring into now, and what I'm seeing is a shallow, selfish idiot. An idiot who only went out with me to get at his sister, to entertain himself by torturing his twin.

And if I've learned *anything* from Mum and Olive and their bad taste in blokes, it's that it's pointless to waste another second on adoring someone who's only going to disappoint me.

"Bye!" I say brightly, wiggling my fingers in his pretty face.

"Huh?" mumbles Marley.

You know something? When this year began, I never expected that my mum would be famous, for good *and* bad reasons.

I didn't expect to meet my dad.

I didn't expect to have a boyfriend.

And I didn't expect that I – the shyest, quietest, least tuneful of the three Brown girls – would get up in front of a couple of hundred people in the Town Hall Square and sing my heart out.

But that's *exactly* what I'm going to do, *right* now.

"Hey, can you help me up?" I ask Freddie.

He grins so wide his smile practically reaches his ears – and immediately drops on to one knee. Like Wolfie before him, he's not proposing to me; he's offering himself as a human step.

And now Mum spots me and holds a hand out as I clamber on to the stage.

"Go Flo!" whoops Freddie, straightening his skinny self up and punching the air.

As I join in with the final chorus – Mum holding my hand, one finger circling my palm – I spot Marley hovering uncertainly, before skulking off into the distance.

And there's Zee, turning to watch him go – before spinning back around and giving me a you-did-the-right-thing nod.

"Thanks!" Mum calls out, as the songs ends and the thundering approval of the audience dies away. "Now I know some of you might recognize me—"

The crowd burst out laughing at her wry understatement.

"—but can I let you in on a secret?" she adds, smile and dimples in full force. "I think losing the *Big Dreams* contest was maybe the best thing that's ever happened to me. Performing with these fantastic ladies? With my gorgeous daughter? It's the most fun I've ever had!"

Cheers erupt from the audience.

From smiling strangers.

From Freddie and Zee, Wolfie and David, Angela and Mario Rossi, Mr and Mrs Chowdri, Bernard and Philip, the three students from above David's office.

From all the lovely Ladies, and Olive and Armando, here on the stage.

Surrounded by our friends and neighbours, I'm sure me and Mum have ended up *just* where we were meant to be.

Not in a big fancy white house in Forest Park, but in Marigold Parade, the street full of roses and cherries and sugar sprinkles on top. . .

JANUARY (*THIS* YEAR)

*Back to how it all ended and
how it all began. . .*

The ad break is over and we're in countdown mode again.

It sounds a little like we might just take off into space.

Which would be a good, if dramatic, way to get out of this studio, and away from smarmy Sasha. . .

During the break I thought she might turn more human, maybe even apologize for going on and on and *on* about the moment Mum "lost it" (her voice, the support of the crowd, her new boyfriend, her record deal, her pride) on live TV.

But instead, Sasha spent the three minutes off air having a) her mask of make-up touched up, and b) a one-sided conversation with the director, talking to her through her earpiece.

". . .Three! Two! *One!*" the young guy with the clipboard finishes off, as the camera swivels around to film our every answer and every squirm.

"Brrrr! It's an icy January morning out there today, isn't it?" Sasha beams at the lens and millions of viewers beyond. "But here at *Rise & Shine*, we have a story that'll melt your hearts . . . a tale of how one woman salvaged a scrap of happiness in the face of total disaster."

Sasha tilts her lollipop head as if she genuinely cares. (Who's she kidding?)

"Yes, after her life literally *fell apart*, Queenie Rae Brown – who lost out at last year's *Big Dreams* final in such a dramatic fashion – is now spending her time teaching a bunch of OAPs to sing!"

Wow . . . Sasha hasn't just patronized Mum, she's also patronized all of Queenie's Choir.

Doesn't she realize that they're all standing in the next studio, waiting to perform, and probably watching this on the monitors? Doesn't she realize how feisty Maureen and Nora and Mrs Georgiou and the others are? And that Olive may well come stomping over here any second and whack Sasha around the head with her plum-coloured handbag?

"I'm very proud of my singers. And very proud of what we've achieved," Mum jumps in and says confidently, before Sasha can wiffle some more stupid remarks about the Ladies.

"Well, yes, from a back street, dilapidated shop to potential stardom!" Sasha laughs, as if it's the most ridiculous thing she's ever heard.

Is she joking?

Marigold Parade is now firmly on the map. The council saw the potential of it being quite the tourist attraction (well, once David stressed it to them) and there are now black and gold signs pointing in our direction from the bus station, from Grey's Road, the Blackwater Retail Park and every which way.

The Ladies are always shrieking at people taking their photos through the window of Armando's with their curlers in. Zee's parents sell loads of the Marigold Parade street sign postcards they had designed. Freddie's folks regularly run out of the Queenie Cakes they make (bog-standard fairy cakes with icing crowns on).

Even Wolfie's doing a nice line in marigold tattoos. Which I have to admit are quite tasteful and pretty. Mum hasn't given in and got one yet – well, as far as I *know*. . .

"The shop's certainly not *dilapidated*, Sasha – it's very much a community space, where we or any other group can perform," Mum says, sounding a little edgy, even if her dimpled smile is out in full force.

"Well, I should hope it's not dilapidated any more, not after all the money you've made from the single," Sasha smiles insincerely. "Number one in the charts for six weeks now? Beating all records for downloads? That's *quite* a little earner."

"Mum's going to use it for charity!" I burst in, in case the watching world thinks Mum is making her fortune out of this.

She's not. With David's help, she's setting up the Marigold Foundation, to get all sorts of choir groups set up in unexpected places: hospices, children's homes and a whole lot more.

Mum's buzzing about it. I've never *seen* her happier. Yep, working with the choir has been Queenie Rae Brown's unexpected happy ending.

That and getting together with David.

Which is something *I* like to take credit for, even if it wasn't deliberate. I'd just decided I'd had enough of secrets, and one day when Mum was chatting about the success of Wolfie's new designs, I told her that she and Wolfie weren't the *only* people on Marigold Parade with tattoos. She was completely blown away when I told her who else had one and exactly what it was.

The next time she saw David, she demanded a peek, and they ended up talking for *hours* about the long-lost days of Queenie's Boys. Next thing, David was showing Mum old photos that he'd scanned in and she was left gasping at the sight of the freckly seventeen-year-old boy, in a woolly hat who'd turned up at every gig. "You were *Beanie!*" she'd laughed, now remembering both David and his once-upon-a-time, pre-accountancy nickname. ("Unless that's what the 'B' stands for in 'D.B. Gregory'!" Wolfie joked when she told him.)

"Yes, of course, Florence," Sasha continues to smarm now. "Anyway, let's take a moment to watch that first-ever performance of Queenie's Choir, shall we?"

The lollipop lady nods towards the monitor once again, and Mum squeezes my hand as we get ready to see the video Wolfie filmed of the Ladies performing their Christmas concert in the Town Hall Square.

It was only a couple of months ago . . . who knew the record companies would immediately come knocking at our door the minute the clip went viral on YouTube? Thank goodness for David, stepping in and managing Mum and the Ladies straight away, before they got bamboozled by silly offers and confusing contracts.

I squeeze Mum's hand back and relax a little. We'll watch the Ladies singing their hearts out, the audience cheering, and then it'll be time for Mum to go to the adjoining studio and lead the choir in a rousing version of "Roses and Cherries", their big hit, and then it'll be thank you and goodbye to Sasha.

As the clip begins, I think for a second about Freddie and Zee; they'll be checking their watches now, both trying to catch as much of Mum and me on *Rise & Shine* before they run to catch the bus to school. Zee will be watching in her flat as Roo crawls in front of the TV, and I bet Freddie will be checking us out on the telly installed on the wall of the Beanz Café.

But hold on. . .

This isn't the clip I was expecting.

Wolfie's video was shot straight on.

This is taken from somewhere at the left-hand side of the watching crowd, with an unsteady hand and the tops of heads in the way. And I'm right there on the left-hand side, nice and close to the built-in microphone of whoever's camera filmed this.

Me, singing Beyoncé's hit nice and loud, *perfectly* out of tune.

As icy fingers of shock and baking shivers of embarrassment zoom up and down my body, I feel Mum clasping my hands tight.

Who did this? I wonder in blind panic. Who filmed this and then thought it would be funny to upload it?

Some stranger, just thinking it was a laugh? Or . . . or maybe Marley, before he skulked off?

"Ha ha ha!" Sasha says over the top of my terrible efforts. "I see you haven't inherited your mother or gran's singing talents, then, Florence?"

For just a hint of a millisecond, I'm tempted to stand up and stomp off-set, but two things stop me: the fact that. . .

a) I'm not sure my suddenly wobbly legs will let me (cue another YouTube blooper: girl trips in a tangle of legs live on air), and

b) one face suddenly comes sharply into focus on the screen. It's Freddie gazing up at me onstage, looking at me *just* the way I've seen David staring at my mum in those old photos he's got. . .

Oh.

And like a lightning flash in my head, I realize that Zee has known how he feels all along; it's why she's been cross with me for stomping on Freddie's feelings without even realizing I've been doing it. It's why she made that comment about the lyrics to Lady Gaga's "Bad Romance" all those months ago, when Freddie was goofing around and serenading me with it.

The thing is, he wasn't goofing. And now I realize I knew all along that "Bad Romance" was about falling for your friend . . . but didn't put two and two – or Freddie and me – together.

"Well, *that* was a bit of fun!" Sasha laughs her mean, twinkly laugh. "But before you go and join your choir, Queenie, I'd just like to thank you and Florence for being *such* good sports this morning on *Rise & Shine*. And who knows what dreams might come true for you girls this year?"

As she speaks, I turn to look directly in the camera.

Out there are millions of people who – for once – *don't* know what's going on in the lives of the Brown girls.

Who don't know that Olive is being trained by

her new best friend Mrs Jennings on how to track people's records online. (She's looking into ways of finding her first husband, so she can finally get a divorce. Otherwise Armando says he'll find someone *else* to marry. "Silly old fool," Olive mutters when he teases her.)

Who don't know that Mum has found her Prince Charming in David. (She's even started styling his wayward sandy hair into something that looks ever so slightly like a quiff.)

Who don't know that Flo Brown is currently staring not at them, but at one particular person.

I smile, and hope that Freddie – my funny, fearless Freddie – gets that my smile is *just* for him.

Like the lollipop lady said, who knows what dreams are in store this year. . . ?

If you enjoyed this, look out for...

Life according to...

Alice B. Lovely

no ordinary nanny

Karen McCombie